"I'm here to spend a little time with my favorite grandmother."

Miz Callie's cheeks flushed. "Your only grandmother, as you well know. Georgia, this is Matthew Harper. Matthew, my granddaughter, Georgia Bodine."

She hadn't identified him as her attorney, and he wondered if the omission was deliberate. He extended his hand again, his eyebrows lifting. Georgia wouldn't refuse it this time unless she wanted open warfare in front of her grandmother.

Georgia took his hand, and he closed his fingers around hers, holding on a bit longer than she'd probably want.

Small, not much taller than her tiny grandmother, Georgia was all softness—soft curves of her body, soft curls in that long, dark brown hair, a soft curve of smooth cheeks. Until you got to her eyes, that is. A deep, deep brown, he guessed they could look like velvet, but they were hard as stone when they surveyed him.

Those eyes issued a warning, but that wouldn't deter him. Fulfilling his client's wishes was a trust to him.

Books by Marta Perry

Love Inspired

A Father's Promise
Since You've Been Gone
*Desperately Seeking Dad
*The Doctor Next Door
*Father Most Blessed
A Father's Place
**Hunter's Bride
**A Mother's Wish
**A Time To Forgive
**Promise Forever
Always in Her Heart
The Doctor's Christmas
True Devotion

†Hero in Her Heart
†Unlikely Hero
†Hero Dad
†Her Only Hero
†Hearts Afire
†Restless Hearts
†A Soldier's Heart
Mission: Motherhood
††Twice in a Lifetime

*Hometown Heroes
**Caldwell Kin
†The Flanagans
††The Bodine Family

Love Inspired Suspense

In the Enemy's Sights
Land's End
Tangled Memories
Season of Secrets
‡Hide in Plain Sight

‡A Christmas to Die For
‡Buried Sins
Final Justice

‡The Three Sisters Inn

MARTA PERRY

has written everything from Sunday School curriculum to travel articles to magazine stories in more than twenty years of writing, but she feels she's found her writing home in the stories she writes for the Love Inspired line.

Marta lives in rural Pennsylvania, but she and her husband spend part of each year at their second home in South Carolina. When she's not writing, she's probably visiting her children and her six beautiful grandchildren, traveling, gardening or relaxing with a good book.

Marta loves hearing from readers, and she'll write back with a signed bookmark and/or her brochure of Pennsylvania Dutch recipes. Write to her c/o Steeple Hill Books, 233 Broadway, Suite 1001, New York, NY 10279, e-mail her at marta@martaperry.com, or visit her on the Web at www.martaperry.com.

Twice in a Lifetime
Marta Perry

Steeple
Hill®

Published by Steeple Hill Books™

STEEPLE HILL BOOKS

Steeple
Hill®

Recycling programs
for this product may
not exist in your area.

ISBN-13: 978-0-373-81425-1

TWICE IN A LIFETIME

Copyright © 2009 by Martha Johnson

www.SteepleHill.com

Printed in U.S.A.

When I look at thy heavens, the work of thy fingers,
the moon and the stars which thou hast established;
what is man, that thou should remember him?
Or mortal man, that thou should care for him?
—*Psalms* 8:3–4

This story is dedicated to my readers, with the hope they will love the Bodine family. And, as always, to Brian, with much love.

Chapter One

Georgia Bodine pulled into the crushed-shell parking space of the aging beach house and got out, the breeze off the ocean lifting her hair and filling her with a wave of courage that was as unexpected as it was welcome. She might be a total failure at standing up for herself, but to protect her beloved grandmother, she could battle anyone.

Couldn't she?

Refusing to let even the hint of a negative thought take hold, Georgia trotted up the worn wooden stairs. The beach house, like most on the Charleston barrier islands, had an elevated first floor to protect against the storms everyone hoped would never come.

The dolphin knocker smiled its usual welcome. The corners of her lips lifted in response, and she rushed through the door, calling for her grandmother as if she were eight instead of twenty-eight.

"Miz Callie! I'm here!"

Her impetuous run took her through the hall and into the large living room that ran the depth of the house. Sunlight pouring through the windows overlooking the Atlantic made her blink.

Someone sat in the shabby old rocker that was her grandmother's favorite chair, but it wasn't Miz Callie.

The man rose, looking as startled by her bursting into the house as she felt finding him here. Aside from the stranger, the room—with its battered, eclectic collection of furniture accumulated over generations and its tall, jammed bookcases—was empty. Where was Miz Callie, and what was this stranger doing here?

The man recovered before she could ask the question. "If you're looking for Mrs. Bodine, she went upstairs to get something. I'm sure she'll be right back."

A warning tingle ran along her skin. The interloper was in his thirties, probably, dressed in a button-down shirt and slacks that were more formal than folks generally wore on Sullivan's Island. He stood as tall as the Bodine men, who tended to height, but tense, as if ready for a fight. Brown hair showed a trace of gold where the sunlight pouring through the window hit it, and his blue eyes were frosty. The few words he'd spoken had a distinctly northern tang.

This was the lawyer, then, the one causing all the trouble. The one who had Uncle Brett muttering about Yankee carpetbaggers and her daddy threatening to call everyone from Charleston's mayor to the South Carolina governor, with a few council members thrown in for good measure. This was— had to be—Matthew Harper.

He took a step toward her, holding out his hand. "I'm Matt Harper. And you are…"

"Georgia Lee Bodine." No matter how rude it was, she would not shake hands with the man. Her fists clenched. "Miz Callie's granddaughter."

Wariness registered in his eyes at the name, and he let his hand drop to his side, his mouth tightening. He knew who she was. Maybe he even knew why the family had called her home from Atlanta in such a rush.

Do something about your grandmother, Georgia Lee. You've always been close. She'll listen to you. You have to talk some sense into her before it's too late.

Who were they kidding? Nobody ever talked Miz Callie out of anything she'd set her mind on. Certainly not Georgia Lee, the least combative of the sprawling Bodine clan.

A flurry of footsteps sounded, and Miz Callie rushed into the room.

"Georgia Lee!"

Georgia barely had time to register a quick impression of her grandmother—five foot nothing, slim and wiry as a girl, white hair that stood out from her head like a halo—before she was wrapped in a warm embrace.

She hugged in return, love rushing through her like a storm tide, and had to blink back tears. Unconditional love, that was what Miz Callie had always offered the shy, uncertain child she'd been, and it was still there for the woman she'd become. Georgia had never been as aware of it as at that moment.

Help me. Her heart murmured a fervent prayer. *Help me keep her safe.*

Over her grandmother's shoulder she stared at Matthew Harper, her determination welling. She had come home because the family said Miz Callie was in trouble—that she was acting irrationally and that this man, this outsider, was trying to con her out of what was hers.

He wouldn't succeed. Not without walking over the prone body of Georgia Lee Bodine, he wouldn't.

Harper's face tightened, as if he could read her mind.

Fine. They knew where they stood, it seemed, without another word being spoken. The battle lines were drawn.

So this was the granddaughter from Atlanta. Matt couldn't help having some preconceived notions about the woman, like it or not, from what he'd seen of Miz Callie and the rest of her family.

He'd already clashed with several members of Miz Callie's large clan over what she planned to do. The two sons he'd spoken to had had the same goal, though they'd gone about it in different ways. Georgia's father, the eldest son, had been all Southern charm and hints of powerful influence, while Brett Bodine, the second of the brothers, intimidating in his Coast Guard uniform, had been blustery and outraged. He hadn't heard from the third brother yet, but no doubt he would.

They hadn't worried him, although he'd been taken aback that Miz Callie's family was so determined to keep her from doing what she wanted with what was hers. Still, he knew, just from the way Miz Callie's face softened when she spoke of Georgia, that this granddaughter had a special place in her heart.

That was undoubtedly why Georgia was here. After failing to influence or intimidate him, the family had sent for her, banking on Miz Callie's affection to sway the decisions she intended to make.

Miz Callie released her granddaughter. "Matthew, I didn't mean to ignore you like that. My manners have gone astray 'cause I'm so excited to see this long-lost granddaughter of mine."

"Miz Callie, you know I was just here at Christmas time." Georgia stood with her arm loosely around her grandmother's waist. Staking out her territory, apparently.

Christmas time? Six months ago, and Atlanta wasn't that far away. If you care so much about your grandmother, Ms. Georgia Lee, why don't you come to see her more often?

"Nice that you could come for a visit, Ms. Bodine." He smiled, sure she'd take that exactly the way he intended. "What brings you back to Charleston— business or pleasure?"

"I'm here to spend a little time with my favorite grandmother."

Miz Callie's cheeks flushed. "Your only grandmother, as you well know. Georgia, this is Matthew Harper. Matthew, my granddaughter, Georgia Bodine."

She hadn't identified him as her attorney, and he wondered if the omission was deliberate. He extended his hand again, his eyebrows lifting. Georgia wouldn't refuse it this time unless she wanted open warfare in front of her grandmother.

Georgia took his hand, holding it as gingerly as if it were a clump of washed-ashore seaweed. He closed his fingers around hers, holding on a bit longer than she'd probably want.

Small, not much taller than her tiny grandmother, Georgia was all softness—soft curves of her body, soft curls in that long, dark brown hair, a soft curve of the smooth cheeks. Until you got to her eyes, that is. A deep, deep brown, he guessed they could look like velvet, but they were hard as stone when they surveyed him.

Those eyes issued a warning, but that wouldn't deter him. Fulfilling his client's wishes was a trust to him.

And on a personal level, he had to succeed at this. He couldn't keep depending on his partner to pull him through. His daughter's face flickered in his mind. For Lindsay's sake, he had to make this work. He was all she had.

"What brought you to Charleston?" Georgia turned his own question back on him. "I can hear from your voice that you're not a native."

"Only of Boston," he said. He doubted she meant the words as a compliment. "I came south to go into partnership with my law-school roommate, Rodney Porter."

Her eyebrows lifted—she obviously recognized the name of an old Charleston family. She couldn't know that Matt was as surprised as anyone at the enduring friendship between the Boston street kid and the Charleston aristocrat, a bond that went back to their first year at Yale.

"I think Rodney was in high school with one of my brothers." Her voice was cool, but he sensed she was giving him a point for that connection.

"I'll have to ask Rod about that."

Her brothers weren't among the family members

he'd met, but they were probably all cut from the same cloth—down-home Southern slow-talkers with a touch of innate courtesy, even when they were castigating him as an interfering outsider who should go back where he came from.

Georgia was different, though—moving at a quicker pace, honed to a sharper edge. Her grandmother had called her a big-city businesswoman. That should make her easier to understand than the rest of her family.

"I'm sure Rodney will remember whether it was Adam or Cole." She smiled. "We all tend to know one another around here."

And you don't belong. That was implicit in her tone, although he didn't think her grandmother caught it.

Georgia wouldn't get under his skin that easily. "You work in Atlanta, I understand. What do you do there?"

"I'm a marketing director for a software firm." Something flickered in her eyes as she said the words, so quickly that he couldn't identify it, but it roused his curiosity. Job problems, maybe?

He'd spun this conversation out as long as possible. Clearly he wouldn't make any progress on Miz Callie's problem today.

He shifted his attention to his elderly client. "Why don't we discuss our business later? After all, your granddaughter has just arrived." In the nick of time, she probably thought.

"I don't want to inconvenience you…" she began.

"I'm sure Mr. Harper will be happy to postpone your meeting," Georgia put in.

Until you've had a chance to try and dissuade your grandmother, he thought.

"That's not a problem." Better to take the initiative than have it taken from him. "I'll give you a call."

"At least take this information with you." Miz Callie picked up a folder she'd dropped on the bookcase when she'd rushed into the room. "It contains the notes I've made on what I want."

Georgia's fingers flexed as if she'd like to snatch that folder. "Maybe we could talk about this first—"

"No." Miz Callie cut her off with what was probably unaccustomed sharpness. "Here you are." She thrust it into his hands.

He took the folder, encouraged by the sign that Miz Callie was set on what she wanted. Maybe Georgia wouldn't find this so easy a task.

"Thank you. I'll go through this and give you a call, then." He turned to go.

As he did, the older woman slipped her arm around her granddaughter's waist again, a look of apology on her face.

Miz Callie knew what she wanted, all right. But if there was one person who could talk her out of it, that person was clearly Georgia Bodine.

* * *

With Harper gone, Georgia's tension level went down a few degrees. She hadn't been able to prevent him from taking away that folder, but whatever business he'd intended hadn't been accomplished yet. She had breathing space to find out exactly what was going on with her grandmother, and how much of her family's wild talk was true.

"You must be hungry." Miz Callie spun and started for the kitchen at her usual trot. "I'll fix you a sandwich, some potato salad—"

"I don't need all that." She followed her grandmother to the kitchen, where African violets bloomed on glass shelves across the windows and a pitcher full of fragrant green basil graced the counter next to the sink.

She closed the refrigerator door her grandmother had opened. "Honestly. I stopped for lunch on the way. Maybe just something to drink. Is there any sweet tea?"

Miz Callie's smile blossomed. "It'd be a sad summer day there wasn't sweet tea in this house. You fill up the glasses with ice."

It was like old times, moving around the kitchen with her grandmother. In moments they'd assembled a tray with glasses, the pitcher of tea, a sprig of mint and a plate of Miz Callie's famous pecan tassies.

Georgia's mouth watered at the sight of the rich,

sweet tarts. Her favorite. But her grandmother hadn't known she was coming, had she?

She'd ask, but Miz Callie was already heading out to the deck off the living room, picking up the battered sun hat she wore outside. Carrying the tray, Georgia followed.

She stepped through the sliding glass door and inhaled the salty scent of sea air. The breeze from the water caressed her skin as it tossed the sea oats that grew thickly on the dunes.

"I love it here." The words came without thought as the endless expanse of sea and sky filled her with a sense of well-being.

Miz Callie gave her characteristic short nod. "Then you understand how I feel." She sat down, reaching out to take Georgia's hand and draw her to the chair next to her. "Stay here at the beach house while you're home, won't you? I'd love to have you."

She hadn't really thought about where she'd stay on this rushed visit, but she could combat whatever Matthew Harper was planning better if she were on the spot.

"I'd love to. I'm sure the folks won't mind."

That was a positive step forward. Now if she could get Miz Callie talking about what the family called her odd behavior…

"You want to tell me what happened to your engagement ring?" Her grandmother's soft voice interrupted her thoughts.

Her gaze flew from Miz Callie to her ring finger. "You noticed." Her mother hadn't, when she'd stopped briefly at the house, and that had been a relief.

"Of course I did, the minute I saw you. What happened with you and James, darlin'?"

One part of her wanted to spill the whole sorry mess into her grandmother's sympathetic ear, the way she would have poured out her problems when she was ten. But she was a grown woman now, and maybe she should act like one.

"It was nothing very dramatic." Wasn't it? A shaft of pain went through her. It hadn't been dramatic only because she lacked the courage to make a scene. "We both realized we'd made a mistake."

She could still see James's face—his amazement that she'd object to his stealing her work, jeopardizing her job and lying about it. The irrevocable differences between them had been shown up as if by lightning.

She forced his image from her mind. "Better now than later, right?"

"That's certain." Her grandmother's clear blue eyes said that she knew there was more. "Still, if you want to talk about it…"

"I know where to come." She pressed Miz Callie's hand.

"Does your mamma know?"

Georgia shook her head. "I'm not looking forward

to that. The day I told her I was engaged was the first time she felt proud of me since I learned to tie my own shoes."

"Oh, sugar, that's not true." Miz Callie looked concerned. "You and your mother don't always see eye to eye about what your life should be like, but she loves you."

The point wasn't that they didn't love each other. She'd just never managed to be the daughter her mother wanted. "I know. I'll tell her."

Just not right away. It was enough that *she* knew her love life was a disaster. Somebody ought to put up poles and orange tape around her to warn others, the way the turtle ladies did around the loggerhead turtle nests on the beach.

"Enough of my sad story," she said. "Tell me what's happening with you."

Her grandmother's eyebrows lifted. "Don't you already know, Georgia Lee? Didn't the family send for you? Tell you that you had to come talk some sense into your foolish old grandmother?"

It was so near to what the family had said that for a moment she couldn't speak. She took a deep breath and sent up a wordless prayer.

"They love you. They don't understand, and they're worried."

"If they don't understand something, they should ask me instead of jumping to conclusions." Miz Callie's voice was as sharp as she'd ever heard it.

Georgia's heart sank. She was used to her father and uncles overreacting to things. But for Miz Callie to take offense—the chasm between them must be bad.

"I'm asking, Miz Callie. They're saying you're giving away things from the Charleston house. That you brought a derelict home for dinner. That you're talking about living here in the cottage year-round all by yourself. Don't you understand how that worries them? You've never done anything like that before."

"Exactly." Miz Callie leaned back, tipping her battered straw sun hat forward. "I'm seventy-five years old, Georgia Lee, and I've spent my whole life doing exactly what other people think I should. I decided it was high time I tried living the way *I* feel I should."

For a moment Georgia couldn't speak again. Miz Callie was the rock in their lives—the one unchanging point. To think that she'd been dissatisfied all that time… She couldn't get her mind around it.

"But you and Grandfather always seemed so happy together."

"Darlin', of course we were happy. I purely loved Richmond Bodine to distraction." Miz Callie's smile eased the tension that was tying Georgia in knots. "I'm not talking about him. I'm talking about society in general. You can't imagine how often I wanted to do somethin' odd, just to shake everyone up."

That feeling she did get. "I always wanted to walk into dancing class in jeans, just to see what would happen."

Laughing, her grandmother took her hand again. "So we're more alike than you thought."

"I'm honored," she said. "But, Miz Callie, bringing a homeless person back to the house— that could be dangerous."

"That poor old man." Her face crinkled in sorrow. "Georgia Lee, that man fought bravely for his country in World War II, and there he was living on the street. I declare, it made my blood boil. Yes, I brought him home, but I called Lola Wentworth— you remember Lola. Her mother, Alma Sue, was a great friend of mine—and she came over and met us. We gave that poor old soul a good meal, and then Lola was able to get him into a decent living situation."

Georgia untangled the digressions into Lola's heritage and realized that the woman must be in social work of some kind. It sounded as if Miz Callie's actions, if unusual, had at least been sensible.

"Did you tell all this to my daddy?"

"I did not." Miz Callie's lips pressed together in a firm line. "He never asked, just started lecturing me as if I were a child."

Her head began to throb. If she'd been hauled home from Atlanta just because her parents and grandmother couldn't sit down and talk things through…

It couldn't be that simple. They hadn't even touched on Miz Callie's move to the cottage, or the rumors of her plans for the property she owned on remote, uninhabited Jones Island, just up the coast.

Or, most of all, how Matthew Harper fit into this.

Chapter Two

Before Georgia could open her mouth to get in her next question, she heard quick, light footsteps on the stairs that led up to the deck from the beach.

"Miz Callie, I found a whelk. Wait 'til you see." A young girl reached the top of the stairs, saw Georgia and stopped. Her heart-shaped face, lit with pleasure, closed down in an instant, turning into a polite, self-contained blank.

The girl reminded Georgia of herself as a child, running to Miz Callie with some treasure. But would she have shut down like that at the sight of a stranger? It was oddly disturbing.

"Lindsay, darlin', how nice. Come here and let me see." Miz Callie held out her hand to the child as she would to coax a shy kitten closer.

The little girl—seven or eight, maybe—shook her head, her blond ponytail flying, blue eyes guarded. "I'll come back later."

"No, no, I want you to meet my granddaughter, Georgia Lee. Why, when she was your age, I believe she loved the beach just as much as you do. Georgia, this is Lindsay."

"Hi, Lindsay." Some neighbor child, she supposed. "I'd love to see your shell, too."

"Come on, sugar." Miz Callie's tender words had the desired effect, and the child crossed the deck to put her treasure in Miz Callie's cupped hands. "It is a whelk. What a nice one—there's not a chip on it."

Georgia blinked, as if to clear her vision. For a moment she'd seen herself, her dark head bent close to Miz Callie's white one, both of them enraptured at what her grandmother would have called one of God's small treasures.

Only when the shell had been admired thoroughly did Miz Callie glance at Georgia again. "Georgia Lee, will you bring out a glass of lemonade for Lindsay?"

She started to rise, but the child shook her head. "No, thank you, Miz Callie. I better go."

Miz Callie's arm encircled the girl's waist. "At least you can have a pecan tassie before you go. I know they're your favorite."

So her grandmother hadn't known she was coming after all. The tassies were for Lindsay.

She smiled at the girl. "Do you live near here, Lindsay?"

Lindsay, faced with a direct question from a stranger, turned mute. Face solemn, she pointed toward the next house down the beach, separated from Miz Callie's by a stretch of sea oats and stunted palmettos.

"We've been neighbors for a couple of months now," Miz Callie said. "Didn't I say? Lindsay is Matthew Harper's daughter."

Georgia's assumptions lifted, swirled around as if in a kaleidoscope and settled in a new pattern. Matt Harper wasn't just a strange attorney picked at random from the phone directory. He was a next-door neighbor, and his daughter was welcomed as warmly as if she were a grandchild, with a plate of her favorite cookies. He was far more entrenched than anyone had seen fit to tell her.

Matt welcomed the breeze off the ocean, even when it ruffled the papers he'd been working on at the table on the deck. He leaned back, frowning.

After looking through her notes, he understood what Mrs. Bodine wanted, but it would be more complicated than she probably suspected. He'd have to deal with a tangle of county, federal and state regulations, many no doubt conflicting.

And that wasn't even counting the opposition of her family. How far were they willing to go to stop her?

He put the folder on the glass table top and weighted it down with a piece of driftwood Lindsay had brought from the beach. He'd start work on the project, and he'd fight it through for Miz Callie. But he'd like to be sure she wouldn't call it off after a talk with Georgia.

Standing, he scanned the beach for Lindsay, not seeing her. She was responsible about staying within the boundaries they'd set up together, which meant that if she wasn't on the beach, she'd gone over to the Bodine house.

He trotted down the steps. He should have mentioned to Lindsay that Mrs. Bodine had a guest. Now he'd have to go over there and retrieve her under Georgia's cool gaze.

The woman had gotten under his skin, looking at him as if he were a con man out to steal a little old lady's treasure. Couldn't the Bodine clan understand that this was all Miz Callie's idea? If he didn't do the work for her, she'd find some other attorney who would.

He couldn't afford that. He didn't intend to sponge off Rodney any longer, accepting the clients Rod managed to persuade to use his new colleague. He needed to bring in business of his own, and Miz Callie's project was the first opportunity he'd had since he and Lindsay moved here.

His steps quickened across the hard-packed sand. He'd taken the chance that this move would be good for Lindsay, a fresh start for both of them. Heaven knew they needed that.

The expression caught him off guard. Once he'd have been praying about this. Once he'd thought the faith Jennifer had introduced him to was strong. But when she died, he'd recognized it for what it was. Secondhand. Nowhere near strong enough to handle a blow like that.

He heard the voices as he reached the stairs to Miz Callie's deck. Three of them: two soft with their Southern drawl, and then his daughter's light, quick counterpoint.

She was talking. It was a sign of how desperate he was about Lindsay's unremitting grief that he didn't care who she was talking to, as long as she talked. At first, after Jennifer's death, the two of them had gone days without saying anything, until he'd realized that he had to rouse himself from the stupor of grief and make an effort for Lindsay's sake.

He went slowly up the steps, hearing the conversation interspersed with gentle female laughter.

"So my brother and I both went under the waves after the shell he'd dropped, but I was the one who came up with it," Georgia said as he reached the top. "Not that I'm suggesting you should do that."

"No, don't, please," he said.

All three of them turned to look at him, but Miz Callie's was the only face that relaxed into a smile. "Matthew, I thought you'd be coming along about now. Come and have some sweet tea."

He shook his head, crossing the deck to them.

There was an empty basket in the center of the table, with shells arrayed around it. His daughter was bent over two shells she seemed to be comparing, ignoring him.

"Lindsay and I need to start some dinner."

"At least take a minute to look at our shell collection. Georgia Lee and I were teachin' Lindsay the names of the different shells."

"Not I," Georgia protested, shoving back from the table. "I'm afraid I've forgotten most of what you taught me."

"You'll have to take a refresher course, won't you?" he said, planting his hands on the back of his daughter's chair.

"How are you at naming the shells of the Carolina coast?" Every time Georgia looked at him, she had a challenge in her eyes.

"Worse than you," he said promptly. "You may have forgotten, but I never knew." He patted Lindsay's shoulder. "Come on, Lindsay. It's time we went home."

"Just a minute. I have to line all the shells up before I go."

He tensed, hating the habit Lindsay had developed, this need to have everything lined up just so. The child psychologist he'd consulted said to go along with it, that when Lindsay's grief didn't require her to seek control in that way, she'd lose interest. But sometimes he wanted to grab her hands and stop her.

A desperation that was too familiar went through him. He'd never known family before Jennifer. Bouncing from one foster home to another hadn't prepared him to be a good father. How could he do this without her?

"How about taking some of these pecan tassies along home for your dessert?" Miz Callie got to her feet, grasping the plate of cookies. "I'll wrap them up for you." She'd headed into the house before he could refuse.

"Don't bother arguing," Georgia said, apparently interpreting his expression. "You can never defeat my grandmother's hospitality. Bodines are noted for being stubborn."

"I've noticed." Something sparked between them on the exchange—maybe an understanding on both their parts that there was a double meaning to everything they said.

She was an interesting woman. If she weren't so determined to believe that he was some sort of legal ogre, he might enjoy getting to know her.

He realized he was looking at her left hand, pressed against the edge of the table. The white band where a ring used to be stood out like an advertisement.

He hadn't given up wearing his wedding ring. Rodney kept pushing him to get into the dating scene, and putting the ring away was the first step. He wasn't ready to do that. What was the point?

There'd never be another Jennifer. A man didn't get that lucky more than once in a lifetime.

The silence had stretched on too long, but surely it was as much Georgia's responsibility as his to break it. He tapped Lindsay's shoulder. "Come on, Lindsay. We'll order in pizza tonight, okay?"

For a moment he thought she'd ignore him, but then Miz Callie came out with the cookies.

"Here you are." She handed the paper plate to Lindsay. "You carry those home and have one for dessert after your supper, y'heah?"

Lindsay got up promptly, good manners surfacing. "I will. Thank you, Miz Callie." She glanced at Georgia, but didn't repeat her thanks. "I'll see you tomorrow."

"That'll be fine, sugar." Miz Callie touched the blond ponytail lightly.

Georgia rose. "I'll walk down with you. I need to get something from my car."

Miz Callie sent her a glance that said she didn't believe a word, but she didn't attempt to deter her. He didn't believe it, either. Georgia had something she wanted to say to him in private.

He followed her down the steps. Lindsay hurried ahead of him along the sand, her gaze fixed on a flight of pelicans overhead. He'd be amazed if those cookies reached home in one piece.

He took a few steps away from the stairs, Georgia moving next to him.

"I didn't realize you lived so close." Georgia's gaze was fixed on his rental. "The Fosters owned that house when I was little. They had five children."

"There are a few kids in the neighborhood now." He watched Lindsay stop and stare at the pelicans as they swooped close to the water. "But Lindsay isn't getting acquainted as easily as I'd hoped. Your grandmother is the only person she's really gotten to know."

"Miz Callie is worth as much as a gaggle of kids any day."

"That sounds like personal experience speaking." Maybe meeting his daughter had softened her attitude toward him.

But she looked at Lindsay, not him. "I was pretty shy as a kid. With my grandmother, there was no pressure. I could play with the other kids if I wanted to, but she never objected to my sitting in the swing with a book, or helping her make cookies in the kitchen."

"Sounds ideal." He spoke lightly, but he thought Georgia had revealed a lot about herself in those few words. Again he had a glimpse of someone he might enjoy getting to know, if not for the fact that she saw him as the enemy.

"I suppose that's how my grandmother came to hire you," Georgia said. "Getting to know you through Lindsay."

"I suppose." He kept it noncommittal. The truce was over already, it seemed.

"Havers and Martin have been the family's attorneys for a couple of generations. It seems a little odd that she came to you instead."

"Does it?" The spark of anger in her eyes amused him.

Her jaw tightened. "I don't believe I heard exactly what it is you're doing for my grandmother."

"You don't really expect me to violate my client's confidence, do you, Ms. Bodine?"

She stopped, her fists clenching, anger out in the open now. "No." She bit off the word. "I don't expect anything from you, Mr. Harper."

She spun and walked quickly back toward the beach house.

Georgia slung her suitcase on the twin bed in the little room under the eaves that had always been hers, the movement edged with the antagonism Matthew Harper had brought out—a quality she hadn't even known she possessed. She'd spent a lifetime unable to confront people, even her own mother. Especially her own mother.

She caught sight of the pale band on her finger in her peripheral vision as she put T-shirts in a drawer. She still had to break that news to Mamma.

Oddly enough, she hadn't had any trouble making her anger clear to Matthew Harper, maybe because she didn't care what he thought of her. Or maybe her love for Miz Callie overrode every other instinct.

Frowning, she shoved the drawer closed. Whatever Matt had in mind, he wouldn't be easily deterred. She'd seen that kind of type A personality in action before. In a way, Matt reminded her of James, although he didn't have her former fiancé's charm. James's smile could make you think he cherished you above all others. The only time it had failed to work on her was when she'd walked out of the office, knowing things were over.

Anyway, this was about Matt, not James. The only time she'd seen any softening in Matt was when he looked at his daughter, and even then his gaze was more worried than loving.

No, she wouldn't be able to dissuade him. She had to find out what Miz Callie had him doing for her before she could learn if her family's suspicions were on target.

She hadn't gotten anywhere with her grandmother over chicken salad and Miz Callie's featherlight biscuits. Dinner had been an elaborate game, with her grandmother determined not to talk about her plans and Georgia equally determined not to talk about her breakup.

Maybe now they could relax and get things out into the open. She took a last look around the room, windows open to the evening breeze, and then hurried down the stairs.

Miz Callie was on the deck, a citronella candle

burning next to her to ward off the bugs. She looked up with a smile as Georgia came out.

"All done unpacking? Did you speak to your mamma and daddy?"

She nodded, not eager to get into what her parents had to say. They'd taken turns talking, Mamma on the extension, so that it had been like being caught between two soloists, both vying desperately to be heard.

"They're fine," she said, knowing Miz Callie wouldn't believe that. She touched the shells on the glass table, still there from her grandmother's impromptu lesson with Lindsay. "Do you want me to put these away?"

"I want you to relax and enjoy." Miz Callie tilted her head back. "Did you ever see so many stars?"

Obediently she leaned back in the chair, staring heavenward, her mind still scrambling for the right way to bring up the things that concerned her. After a moment or two, the tension began to seep out of her. How could anyone sit here surveying the darkened sea and the starlit sky and fret? The surf murmured softly, accompanying the rustling of the palmetto fronds and the sea oats.

"I don't even notice the stars in Atlanta. Too many city lights."

Miz Callie made a small sound of contentment. "They seem to put us in our places, don't they? 'When I look at the heavens which Thou has created, the moon and the stars, which Thou hast ordained, what is man that Thou are mindful of him, or the son of man, that Thou visiteth him?'"

Her grandmother's gentle voice brought a lump to her throat. "That's always been one of your favorite psalms, hasn't it?"

Miz Callie nodded, and the silence grew comfortably between them. Finally she spoke again, eyes still on the night sky. "I am worried about that child."

The change of subject startled her. "You mean Lindsay?"

"She's so withdrawn. You must have noticed how she was when she saw I had someone here."

"She's probably just shy." She knew how that felt.

"Grief." Miz Callie moved slightly, hand reaching out to the glass of sweet tea beside her. "The child's still grieving her mother's death."

So Matt was a widower. She hadn't been sure, since he still wore a wedding ring, but it had seemed implicit in the interactions with his daughter.

"Maybe he was wrong to take her away from everything that was familiar to her, just for the sake of his career."

Miz Callie turned to look at her in the dim light. "Georgia Lee, you don't know a thing about it, so don't you go judging him."

When Miz Callie spoke in that tone, an apology was in order. "No, ma'am. I'm sorry."

Her grandmother's expression eased. "I suspect he felt it was time for a fresh start. Sometimes that happens."

"Sometimes a fresh start is forced on you." What was she going to do after this interlude? Go back to Atlanta and try to find another job?

"And sometimes you just know it's the right time."

Something in her grandmother's tone caught her attention. "Is that why you want to move to Sullivan's Island permanently? Because you want a fresh start?"

Miz Callie waved her arm. "Who wouldn't want to live here, simply, instead of being enslaved to a lot of *things?*" She said the word with emphasis.

"So that's why you've been giving stuff away at the Charleston house." A frightening thought struck her. "Miz Callie, you're not dying, are you?"

For a moment her grandmother stared at her. Then her laugh rang out. She chuckled for several moments, shaking her head. "Oh, child, how you do think. We're all of us dying, some of us sooner than later, but no, there's nothing wrong with me."

"Then why…"

Her grandmother sighed, apparently at Georgia's persistence. "Do you remember Mary Lyn Daniels?"

Georgia's mind scrambled among her grandmother's friends and came up with an image. "Yes,

I think so. She's the one you always say has been your friend since the cradle, isn't she?"

"Was," Miz Callie said. "She passed away this winter."

"I'm sorry." She clasped her grandmother's hand, aware of the fragility of fine bones covered thinly by soft skin. She should have known about that. She would have, if she'd come back more often. "Did Mary Lyn's death—is that what has you thinking of making so many changes?"

Her grandmother smiled faintly. "This isn't just about grieving my friend, darlin'. At my age, I've learned how to do that. I know I'm going to see them again."

"What then?" She leaned toward her, intent on getting answers. "There must be some reason why you feel such a need to change things."

Miz Callie stared out at the waves. "I'd go and sit with Mary Lyn, most afternoons. Seemed like all she wanted to do was talk about the old days, when we were children here on the island. Her memory of those times was clearer than what happened yesterday."

"I'm sorry you had to go through that." She choked up at the thought of Miz Callie sitting day after day with her dying friend. Small wonder if it made her reflect on her own mortality.

"It was good to sit there with her and remember those years." Miz Callie's tone was soft, far away.

"But sometimes she'd start in on things she regretted. Old hurts never mended. Relationships lost." She shook her head slowly. "I don't want to be like that at the end. And I'm thinking maybe God used Mary Lyn to show me it's time to right old wrongs and make my peace with life."

"Miz Callie, I don't believe you ever did anything that needs righting." She hadn't been ready for a conversation about life and death tonight, and she was swimming out of her depth. "If that's why you want to move here to the island full-time, I can understand, but I know there's more. That doesn't explain you hiring an attorney nobody knows to handle business no one knows about."

Miz Callie sighed, suddenly looking her age and more. Then she leaned over to put her hand on Georgia's.

Georgia clung to that grip: the hand she'd always held, the one that had reassured her as a child. Now it felt cool and delicate in hers.

"All right, Georgia Lee. I know you're worrying about me. Tomorrow."

"Tomorrow what?" she asked, confused.

"Matt is comin' tomorrow to meet with me. You can sit in with us. I'll explain everything then."

"But, Miz Callie…" She didn't want to wait. And she certainly didn't want to hear about it—whatever it was—in front of Matt.

"Tomorrow." Her grandmother's voice was tired

but firm. "I'm not goin' over it twice, sugar, and that's that. You'll hear all about it then."

Georgia clamped her lips shut on an argument. Tomorrow. She'd have to be content with that.

Chapter Three

Georgia sat in line for the drawbridge leading back onto Sullivan's Island, glancing at her watch as if that would help. She'd be late for the meeting with Matt if she didn't get moving, and she didn't want Miz Callie to say anything to him that she wasn't there to hear.

It was a good thing Miz Callie had reminded her to bring the cooler for the groceries. The closest supermarket was in Mount Pleasant, across the Cooper River from Charleston proper, across the Intracoastal Waterway from Sullivan's Island. Not far, but not just around the corner, either, so islanders tended to stock up when they went.

At least once she got to the house, the secrecy would be over. Miz Callie would come clean with her so that she could resolve this situation, whatever it was, and get back to her own life, whatever was left of it.

A tall sailboat moved serenely past, and the bridge lowered into place. With a sigh of relief, she rumbled across the bridge and back onto the island. Right, then left, then left again, and she pulled up to the house.

She went up the stairs slowly, laden down by the many bags of groceries she was attempting to take in one trip. She fumbled with the door, staggered in and found that Matt was already there.

He rose, coming quickly to help her with the bags, his dress shirt and dark tie reinforcing the fact that this was a business visit and not a neighborly call.

"Where do you want these?" He followed her into the kitchen.

She nodded toward the counter. "Let me put things in the refrigerator, and then I'll join you." She waited for an argument from him, but none came.

"Good. I think you should be in on this."

He sounded sincere enough. Or maybe he was just accepting what he couldn't change. She slid the milk and a bag of perishables onto the shelves and closed the fridge. Then she followed Matt into the living room.

Papers were spread across the round table where she and her girl cousins used to play with their paper dolls. She sat down in the wicker chair opposite Miz Callie.

Now that the moment had come, she wasn't at all sure she wanted to find out what this was all about.

She glanced at Matt, but he wore his stolid lawyer's expression that didn't give anything away.

Miz Callie sat very straight in her rocker, hands folded in her lap. "I've made a decision about the Jones Island property. I'm afraid it won't be popular with the family, but my mind is made up, and there's no point in arguing about it."

"I'm not going to argue, Miz Callie." The piece of property on the uninhabited small barrier island had come down to Miz Callie through her side of the family. It was hers to do what she liked with. Surely she realized nobody would contest that.

"Good." Her grandmother gave a short nod. She sounded very much in control, but Georgia could see her hands were clasped tightly to keep them from trembling. "Matthew is going to turn the Jones Island land into a nature preserve to protect it from ever being developed."

Georgia blinked. Whatever she'd expected, it hadn't been this, not after all the secrecy. "Do you mean you're turning it over to the state?"

"Nothing so simple," Matt said. "Miz Callie wants the land in a private trust, so that she controls what's done there. That makes it considerably more difficult to navigate all the various governmental regulations."

"You're doing fine." Miz Callie waved away the issue. "It'll be exactly the way I want it."

This was a tempest in a teapot, as far as she could

tell. "Miz Callie, whatever has all the secrecy been about? You must know that no one in the family will object to turning the land into a nature preserve."

"Yes, child, I know that." Miz Callie's face seemed to tighten, as if the skin were drawing close against the bones. "They won't object to the preserve. They'll object to what I'm going to call it."

"Call it?" Georgia echoed. This was like swimming in a fog.

Her grandmother continued to clasp her hands tightly together. "It's to be named the Edward Austin Bodine Memorial Preserve."

For a moment the name didn't register. Then memories filtered through—of pictures quickly flipped past in the family album, of questions unanswered, of conversations broken off when a child entered the room.

"You mean Great-uncle Ned? Grandfather's older brother? The one who—" She stopped, not sure how much of what she thought she knew was true and how much was a child's imagining.

"They said he was a coward. They said he ran away rather than defend his country in the war." Her grandmother's cheeks flushed. "It wasn't true. It couldn't have been."

Georgia caught the confusion in Matt's eyes. "The Second World War, she means. Supposedly Ned Bodine disappeared instead of enlisting when he was old enough to fight." She tried to think this through, but her instinctive reaction was strong. "Miz Callie, you must know it's not only the family who will be upset about this idea. Other folks have long memories, too. Why don't you dedicate it to Grandfather?"

"To Ned." Her voice was firm. "He's been the family secret for too long."

"Will people really be upset after all this time?" Matt asked. "Would anyone even remember?"

The fact that Matt could ask the question showed how far he had to go in understanding his adopted home.

"They remember. Charleston society is like one big family with lots of branches. Everyone knows everyone else's heritage nearly as well as they know their own." She ran her fingers through her hair, tugging a little, as if that would clear her thoughts. "And it's not just that. This is a military town, always has been. Bodines have served proudly." Her mind flickered to her brothers. "Miz Callie, please rethink this."

Her grandmother shook her head firmly. Tears shone in her eyes.

Georgia's heart clenched. Miz Callie was the rock of the family. She didn't cry. She didn't show weakness. And she certainly didn't do things that would put half the county in an uproar.

Except…now she did.

She reached across to grasp her grandmother's trembling hands. "It's going to cause a lot of hard feelings, you know."

Miz Callie clutched her hand, her gaze seeking Georgia's face. "Not if it's proved that he didn't run away."

"After all this time? Miz Callie, if people have believed that all these years, surely it must be true. I know you were fond of him, but—"

"I knew him." The words came out firmly. "He wasn't a coward, whatever people say."

"Please, think about what will happen if you do this." Her grandmother was set on a course that would hurt her immeasurably. "Even if you're right, how can you prove it after all these years?"

"Maybe I can't, not alone." Her fingers tightened on Georgia's. "I want you to help me."

"Me?" The word came out in an uncertain squeak.

"I can't die without making this right. I should have done it long ago."

The echo of something lost reverberated in her words, twisting Georgia's heart. So this was the wrong she'd talked about—the one that needed righting.

"Miz Callie, you know I'd do anything for you. But I wouldn't know where to begin."

"Matthew will help you. The two of you can do it. You have to." Her voice didn't waver, but a tear spilled down her cheek.

Georgia's throat tightened as panic swept through her. How? The one thing her grandmother asked of her, and she couldn't even think where to begin.

She turned to Matt and saw the reluctance in his eyes. He was no more eager to take this on than she was, even though he didn't understand the situation the way she did.

As for the family—her stomach clenched at the thought of explaining this to them. It made her want to scurry back to Atlanta until the storm was over.

But she couldn't, because the bottom line was, if she couldn't talk Miz Callie out of this, she also couldn't leave her to face the consequences alone.

"All right." She patted her grandmother's hand. "You win. I'll do my best."

As to whether that would be good enough—well, she seriously doubted it.

Georgia tiptoed out onto the deck when the sun was still low over the ocean, her running shoes in her hands. Miz Callie was sleeping, and she didn't want to disturb her, but an early morning run was just what she needed to clear her mind.

She tugged the laces tight. After a night of trying to think of a good way to explain the situation to her parents, she didn't have an answer. Too bad she wasn't more like her cousin Amanda, the older of Uncle Brett's and Aunt Julia's twins. Amanda never let anyone stand in her way when she was convinced she was right. Of course, that led to the kind of loud arguments that would have Georgia hiding under the bed, but at least Amanda fought for what she wanted.

Well, she wasn't like Amanda and never would be. And their grandmother wasn't turning to Amanda right now. She was turning to Georgia, and it was up to her to do the right thing for Miz Callie.

Once she knew what that was, anyway. She trotted down the stairs and stopped abruptly, halfway down. "Adam!"

Her oldest brother held out his arms when he saw her, and she catapulted into them for a hug that lifted her off her feet.

"Hey, Little Bit, how are you?"

"Don't call me that," she said automatically, though she doubted she'd ever get him to stop, since he'd been teasing her with that since their parents brought her home from the hospital.

"Pardon me, Ms. Georgia Lee." He set her down, grinning. "I just have trouble believing you're all grown up now, and engaged to boot."

She focused on his chest, clad in a Coast Guard Academy T-shirt, instead of his face. She couldn't fool Adam. "That last part's not so true anymore."

"Really?"

She nodded, miserably aware that the news could now be spread to her huge extended family in a matter of minutes. "Listen, Adam, you can't tell anybody the engagement's over. I didn't tell Mamma yet."

He whistled softly. "Okay. Nobody's hearin' it from me, cross my heart. But you probably ought to tell her soon."

"I know. But you know how she'll be, denied the prospect of a wedding. I don't suppose you'd care to get married instead." She peeped up at his face, ready for his grin.

"Not me," he said quickly. "This old boy is not putting his head into a noose, thank you very much."

She shook her head with mock sorrow. "What are you doing over here this early? On your way to or from the station?"

Adam, like his father and many other family members, had gone into the Coast Guard almost automatically. That was what Bodines did. He seemed to thrive on the life. His lean, craggy face lit up whenever anyone gave him a chance to talk about the service.

"I'm on duty in an hour, but I figured I'd catch you jogging and get in a private chat." He glanced toward the cottage. "How's Miz Callie?"

"Fine. Feisty as ever."

"You find out what's going on with her yet?"

She hesitated. The last thing Miz Callie had said to her the previous evening was a plea to keep this quiet, at least for a while, from the family. She'd tell them when she was ready. And maybe, just maybe,

Georgia could get her to forget the whole naming thing before anyone exploded.

"Here's the thing." It looked as if she could practice on Adam, who was bound to be more receptive than the older generation. "We talked a little, and honestly, she seems to have logical reasons for most of the things that have the parents so upset."

"Stands to reason Daddy and Uncle Brett and Uncle Harrison would overreact. They always do egg each other on."

Like you and Cole. Their middle sibling piloted a Coast Guard jet in Florida, intercepting drug runners and potential terrorists. It was dangerous, much as Daddy played that down.

"Still." His lean face was troubled. "There's been talk about the property over on Jones Island. You probably don't know, being up to Atlanta so much, but prices on the barrier islands have skyrocketed lately. Jones Island won't be uninhabited much longer."

She shrugged, since there was nothing she could safely say on that subject. "That land does belong to Miz Callie, after all. Came down in her family, not Granddad's, not that it makes much difference."

"Well, sure, I don't care what she does with it. I just don't want to see some shady lawyer cheating her over it, if she's decided to sell."

"We don't know that he's shady." An image of Matt's face formed in her mind. Tough, workaholic, stubborn and inexorable as the tide. But shady? Even on short acquaintance, she found she doubted that.

"We don't know what she's doing." Adam sounded frustrated. "That's what's driving everyone crazy. Haven't you found out anything yet?"

"I've barely gotten settled in," she reminded him. "And she is talking to me. If everyone would just give us a little time, I'm sure things will settle down." She hoped.

He slung his arm around her shoulders and hugged her, as if he heard the uncertainty that clung to her. "Sorry, Little Bit. I didn't mean to fuss at you. But the folks…"

"Well, since you won't get married to rescue me from their disapproval, could you at least convince them I need a little time? Get them to stop calling me for a progress report every few hours."

"Guess I can do that much for you." He planted a kiss on her cheek. "I'll try to head them off, but sooner or later—"

"I know. But Miz Callie's got her back up. I'd just as soon we not start a family fight over this."

"You've got your work cut out for you, sugar." He tugged at her ponytail. "I'd better get going. It's good to have you here, you know, instead of way up in Atlanta."

"It's good to see you." A wave of love for her big

brother swept over her. She threw her arms around him in a hug, then stepped back, feeling better.

He grinned, winking at her. "Later." He went off at an easy lope.

She turned, looking out at the beach. Apparently she wasn't the only person who liked an early morning run. Matt Harper jogged slowly past the house, his gaze fixed on her as if wondering whom she'd been talking to—and why.

It was late afternoon after a frustrating workday when Matt crossed the sand to where Miz Callie sat. The tide was out, and the beach, glistening and empty, invited him. It had been a relief to change out of office clothes and step outside to this.

"Miz Callie." He nodded to his daughter, who was in the surf with Georgia. "I hope Lindsay's not being a pest."

"Not at all." She tilted the brim of her straw sun hat back to look at him. "Georgia needed someone to play with, and your housekeeper had some laundry to finish up."

"Georgia might not like hearing you refer to her as if she were about eight," he said, and Miz Callie chuckled.

Lindsay was batting a red and white-striped beach ball to Georgia. Knee-deep in the water, she looked more relaxed and open than he'd seen her in months.

"They've been having a good time." Miz Callie was watching them, too, and her face curved with a reminiscent smile. "It's like old times, having Georgia here."

"It must have been a circus when all your grandchildren were young."

"My land, yes." Her smile broadened. "What one of them didn't think of, the others did. Seems like only yesterday they were all children, romping on the beach, and now they're grown up, with lives of their own."

And too busy to spend time with their grandmother? He wondered if that were the case. If so, she probably wouldn't say. It would seem disloyal to her.

"At least you have Georgia back for a while."

Until he and Georgia figured out what to do about the memory of Ned Bodine. He'd hoped to have the chance to start a preliminary search today, but Rod had called him in to help with another client. He and Georgia really needed to sit down and talk through how they were going to approach this, little though she might want to work with him.

"Why don't you get into the game? I'm sure Lindsay would like that."

"Good idea." And maybe he could get a moment or two with Georgia to make some plans. Pulling off his T-shirt, he ran across the wet sand to the water.

Georgia threw the beach ball to Lindsay, but the breeze took it, lifting it out of her reach. He grabbed it.

Lindsay charged toward him, animated. "Me—throw it to me!"

He tossed the beach ball to her, and she threw it to Georgia. Georgia hesitated a moment, clutching the ball. Her damp hair curled around her face, and sunlight glinted off her skin.

"Maybe your dad wants to take over the game now," she suggested.

"No, no!" Lindsay jumped up and down in the water. "Don't quit now, Georgia."

"Don't quit now, Georgia," he echoed. He looked at her with a challenge in his gaze. She surely wouldn't stop playing with his child just because he was there.

"All right." Her smile lit. "We have three, so we can play Monkey in the Middle. My brothers always made me be the monkey first, because I was the smallest. So that's you, Lindsay."

"I can jump high." She bounced, facing Georgia and waving her arms.

"Here goes." Georgia didn't make it easy for Lindsay, tossing it well over her head on the first throw. But a couple of tosses later, she threw the ball a little low, and Lindsay grabbed it.

"You're the monkey," she said, giggling.

For a moment his eyes misted. How long had it

been since he'd heard that giggle? How long since he and Lindsay had really played together?

They batted the ball back and forth, keeping it away from Georgia even though she lunged for it as if she were a kid again. When she almost succeeded, he made a dive and grabbed it away just as her fingers touched it.

"No fair." She splashed him. "My brothers always did that, too, because they're taller than I am."

"You're mad because Lindsay and I are so good at this game." He tossed it to his daughter, loving the sound of her laugh, wondering again why he hadn't thought of doing something as simple as this.

Jennifer had always taken the initiative with Lindsay, planning their family time with meticulous care, perhaps because it was so limited. He'd put all of his energy into his career, determined to take good care of them.

But he hadn't been able to protect Jennifer from the cancer that stole her away, and now he had to find a way of doing all the things she'd have done with Lindsay.

Maybe because he was distracted, he tossed the ball too low, and Georgia grabbed it. She held it aloft triumphantly. "Lindsay and I are going to get you now."

He moved to the middle, and she tossed the ball

to his daughter. Biding his time, he waited until Georgia got a little too confident, then leaped for the ball.

He started to pull it down when Georgia jumped, batting at the ball. She almost got it, lost her footing and went splashing down into the water.

He caught her arm and pulled her to her feet. She surfaced laughing, water streaming down her face, her head a riot of curls. He took hold of her other arm to steady her until she got her balance.

Her gaze met his, the brown eyes just as velvety as he'd imagined they might be. She seemed to glow with life and vitality. Her gaze grew wider, more vulnerable, and for an instant the world compressed into the sunlight, the sea and Georgia.

"Who was he?" The question came out before his brain was in gear. "The man you were hugging the other morning. Your fiancé?"

"My brother. Adam." She didn't seem to question his right to know. "How did you know about my fiancé?"

In answer he held up her left hand, water sheeting off it. The white line was growing fainter after several days at the shore, but it was still visible.

"Your grandmother mentioned you were engaged but the ring isn't there now."

She nodded. "I don't expect to be seeing him here. Or anywhere."

Good. That was what he wanted to say. But why

should it make any difference to him who she hugged?

He fought to focus on business. "We need to get together to make some plans." He said the words quietly, glancing toward Miz Callie. "Soon."

Georgia's face tightened a little, but she nodded. "Right. I can come over this evening if you want. After Lindsay goes to bed."

He almost asked her to come to the office, but that would seem foolish when they were neighbors. He couldn't let his actions be affected by...well, by the attraction that had blindsided him, like a wave crashing into him when he wasn't looking. Attraction to Georgia was a mistake, best ignored.

"Around eight-thirty, then."

Lindsay chose that moment to hurl the ball at them with all her might, cutting off anything else he might have said.

He turned away. Georgia did, too. But he sensed that she, too, was aware that things had shifted between them in some incalculable way.

Chapter Four

Someone who hadn't grown up here might find it scary to be walking on the beach at night. Not Georgia. She used a shielded flashlight through the dunes, but when she reached the flat expanse of sand, she switched it off. The nearly full moon traced a silvery path across the waves, so distinct that when she was a child, she'd imagined that if only she were brave enough, she could walk on it all the way to the horizon and beyond.

She knew better now, but that didn't detract from the beauty. Miz Callie's favorite psalm surfaced in her mind, like a dolphin breaking through the waves.

When I look at the Heavens, which Thou hast created, the moon and the stars, which Thou hast ordained...

She tilted her head back to study the sweep of

the stars. She felt small in the face of that vastness. Insignificant. And wasn't that what the psalm went on to say?

What is man, that Thou art mindful of him, or the son of man, that Thou visiteth him? Yet Thou hast made him a little lower than the angels, and crowned him with glory and honor.

The words created a space of peace in her heart, like the walk on the beach. The distance between Miz Callie's house and Matt's place gave her time to think about what she would say to him. Unfortunately, she couldn't seem to think of much except those moments in the surf earlier.

Where had that instant wave of attraction come from? It was crazy. Neither of them wanted that. What was she supposed to do now—pretend it hadn't happened?

The night, in its stillness, didn't provide an answer, but the murmur of the surf soothed away the edge of her anxiety. She was worrying over nothing. Matt would be as eager to forget it as she was.

Crossing the dunes to Matt's deck, she slipped on the shoes she'd been carrying and walked up the steps to find him waiting for her.

"I saw you coming down the beach." He gestured to a chair, waited until she took it, and sat down next to her.

She perched on the edge of the chair, too aware of his nearness to relax.

Even in the dim light, she could see his eyebrows lift. "You look as if you're ready to take flight. Is something wrong?"

"No, not at all." If she couldn't convince herself, at least she could try convincing him. "Is Lindsay asleep?"

"She conks out pretty quickly. I guess she wears herself out running around on the beach all day."

"I remember that feeling."

He'd spend most of his evenings alone, once Lindsay went to bed. That must be lonely.

"Well, to business." He drained his iced-tea glass and set it on a wide plank of the deck. "We need a plan of action, don't you think?"

"I suppose." Tension grabbed the back of her neck. "The trouble is—well, truthfully, I don't see how this can succeed. I'm afraid Miz Callie will end up being hurt if she can't clear Ned's name. And if she goes ahead with her plans anyway..." She trailed off.

He rubbed the back of his neck, as if he felt the same stress she did. "Will there really be that much bad feeling after all this time?"

She gave him a pitying look. "You don't get it, do you? Charleston—old Charleston, anyway—is a close community for all its size. I don't suppose anyone will start a petition against her plans, although that could happen. But people she's known all her life will disapprove, even be angry about it."

"Maybe she figures that won't bother her."

"Don't kid yourself. She may say that she wants to live to please herself, but I know her. She'll be lost if people turn against her. Lost."

"You know her better than I do." He paused, his face a study in line and shadow in the dim light. "But as her attorney, I have to follow her directions."

She hadn't known him long, but she sensed instinctively that he wouldn't back away from his duty to a client. "Any ideas?"

"Miz Callie must have some reason for her belief in Edward Bodine's innocence. You're in the best position to find out what that is."

"I guess so. I tried to find out what she remembers about his leaving, but it's not much. Just finding Granddad crying because Ned had run away, leaving a note saying he wasn't coming back, but that's all she knows. Maybe it was all Granddad knew. After all, he was just a kid then, too."

"If he left a note saying he was going, there was no question of accident or foul play, apparently."

She blinked. "That hadn't even occurred to me. But no, I suppose not. I can try to get her talking more about her memories. There might be something we can follow up on."

He nodded. "Good. And there have to be records of Edward Bodine somewhere. I'll start there, see what that tells us."

"If there's something else I can do…"

"There is," he said, so promptly that it seemed he was waiting for the offer. He picked something up from the floor next to his chair, and she realized it was a long legal pad. "I just have too little information to search intelligently. That's where you come in."

She should not be annoyed that he was so quick to take charge. She shouldn't, but she was.

She shoved the feeling down. Her grandmother was important now, not her. "What do you need me to find out?"

"Vital statistics, like birth date, parents' names, addresses." He ticked something off on the pad. "And anything you can get from your grandmother about how and when he disappeared. Why did people think he ran away?" His hand tightened into a fist. "It's all just so amorphous. A story that's more than sixty years old and not a single fact to support it."

"It's about more than facts. There's family loyalty and trust involved, too."

"I can't investigate family loyalty." His voice had gone dry, his hand tight on the arm of the chair. "Just get me some facts. Surely your grandmother remembers more than she's told us so far."

Was that just a normal lawyer's reaction, his insistence on sticking to the facts? Or did she sense something deeper in his reaction to her comment about families?

"Miz Callie did say she's started remembering more about that summer. Apparently she'd been talking with a friend from those days, reminiscing."

"Who is the friend?" His question was quick, his pen poised over the legal pad. "Maybe we can interview him."

"Her. And we can't. She died." She sounded as terse as he did.

"I'm sorry. I didn't mean to upset you." He reached across the space between their chairs to touch her hand lightly.

Her skin tingled at his featherlight touch. She shoved her hair back from her face with her other hand, looking up at the stars again. They seemed very far away.

"It's all right. I'm not personally upset about her death. I mean, I barely remember her. But her passing had a profound effect on my grandmother. That's what convinced her she has to learn the truth about Ned."

"I see." His fingers brushed hers lightly, as if in silent empathy. "One other thing—what about talking to your family about Ned?"

She winced at the thought. "Miz Callie is right to put that off as long as possible."

"I suppose they wouldn't be pleased."

"Pleased?" Her voice rose in spite of herself and she half expected him to pull his hand away, but he didn't. The warmth of his skin began to radiate through her. "You've seen how they reacted already. If they knew this… Trust me, you don't want to see the Bodines in full crisis mode."

"I think I could handle it." He said the words mildly. But then, he wasn't related to them.

"It would only make matters worse, and my dad's generation won't know any more than Miz Callie does."

"All right. If you say so." He seemed to become aware that he was still touching her hand. He grasped the legal pad instead. "We'll work it out, somehow."

"I hope so." It was odd, talking to him this way, relying on him when she barely knew him. More than odd, to feel lonely because he was no longer touching her.

He cleared his throat. "Anyway, you'll try to get a bit more information from your grandmother. Do you think there's anyone else we might talk to about that summer?"

She forced herself to concentrate. "I'll try to find out." She rose, and Matt stood with her.

"Thanks." He looked down at her, his gaze searching her face.

She sucked in a breath. "Good night, Matt." She turned quickly, before he could answer, and hurried down the stairs, her skin still tingling from his touch.

Her mind still occupied with the conversation with Matt as she came back from her run the next morning, Georgia went up the steps to the deck and met her grandmother coming out. The floppy hat, oversized floral shirt and cutoffs were Miz Callie's typical summer outfit. Her red plastic pail represented one of her most prized roles—that of an island turtle lady.

"Miz Callie, you're not going out without breakfast, are you?" She glanced through the glass door, seeing only a coffee mug on the kitchen table.

Her grandmother slid a pair of pink-rimmed sunglasses on her face. "I had coffee. That's all I need now. I'll eat something when I get back from my patrol."

"Why don't you let me fix you some scrambled eggs first?" And talk to me while you're eating. "Surely the turtles can wait that long."

"Georgia Lee, I've been taking care of myself for a good long time, and I don't intend to stop in the foreseeable future." She walked toward the stairs, the red pail swinging. "'Course, you could come along with me to look for nests."

She was just as likely, or unlikely, to get something out of her grandmother on the beach as anywhere else. She followed her toward the beach.

"It's early in the season, isn't it? Have you found any nests so far?"

"Well, it's May already." Miz Callie set off along the dunes. "We haven't found any on Sullivan's

Island yet, but they've spotted quite a few over at the national seashore. And two on Isle of Palms."

There was the faintest thread of envy in her grandmother's voice. She, like the rest of the turtle ladies, wanted to be the first one to spot the marks that showed a turtle had nested in the dunes, depositing her eighty or more eggs in the sand.

"Maybe today will be your lucky day," she said. "For finding a nest, I mean."

Miz Callie smiled as her gaze scanned the dunes. "I'd purely love that, to find a turtle nest with you. It's been a long time—maybe since that summer before you went off to college."

Georgia's mind slid automatically away from the memory of that summer. *Don't think about that. Remember other times, happier times.*

She tilted her head back, loving the warmth of the sun on her face, the scent of the sea teasing her nose. "I'd forgotten how much I love this place." The note of surprise in her voice caught her off guard.

"You always did, from the time you were a little bitty child." Her grandmother slowed, as if she didn't have quite enough breath for both walking and talking. "You should come more often. Why did you stop?"

Again her mind shied away from the memory she'd never shared with her grandmother. "I got older. Life got complicated."

"It does. Believe me, I know. Are you so surprised that I want to simplify it now?"

"I guess not." Except that this quest her grandmother had embarked on was likely to provide plenty of complications. Didn't she realize that? Maybe she did, and she just wanted the other parts of her life settled so she could save her strength for the battle over Ned's name.

Miz Callie stopped, staring at the gentle ruffle of the waves. The tide was going out, leaving long, shallow tidal pools behind—a favorite playground for children. In an hour or two, they'd start appearing on the beach, little family parties of a mother or a set of grandparents laden down with chairs, umbrellas, maybe a cooler, ready for a few hours on the beach with the kids. The air would fill with the excited voices of the young.

"We fall into the rhythm of the ocean when we're born here," Miz Callie said softly, almost as if she were talking to herself. "Maybe that's why Bodines never really thrive away from the sea."

Her grandmother had a point. Her brothers had followed the family tradition and gone into the Coast Guard. They couldn't conceive of a life that didn't involve the sea.

"We all love this place," Georgia said. "But still…"

Miz Callie stiffened. She wasn't reacting to Georgia's words. In fact, it was doubtful that she'd even heard them.

She stared, taking off her sunglasses and shielding her eyes with her hand. Georgia looked, too, scanning sand, sea oats and morning glories for the telltale signs.

"There!" Miz Callie pointed and scurried toward the spot. "It might be a nest!"

She spotted it now—the tracks in the sand leading to the dunes, as if a small tractor had gone through. Georgia hurried after her grandmother, Miz Callie's enthusiasm infectious. She was thirteen or fourteen again, running after her grandmother, sharing the thrill of being first to find a viable nest.

"She's picked a good site." Miz Callie lowered herself to her knees next to a patch of disturbed sand. "Well above the high-tide line, thank goodness."

If it hadn't been, the volunteers would have taken on the risky task of moving the nest farther back. That would be the only chance the babies had of surviving. It was all coming back to her.

Georgia knelt beside her grandmother. "Are there eggs in it?" That was the crucial question. The mother could have been frightened away before she'd finished the job.

"Only one way to find out." Miz Callie took a long, thin stick from the pail. Slowly, her face intent, she inserted it into the sand, probing delicately for the eggs.

Her grandmother's expression touched Georgia's

heart. Miz Callie's love for the sea creatures native to this coast went so deep. It was an act of faith for her, a part of her reverence for all that God had created.

Georgia made herself comfortable on the dune. This could take a while, and she knew better than to offer help. Miz Callie had never let any of the grandchildren touch the precious eggs. If the grandkids were lucky, they'd be roused from sleep some night and taken out on the beach. Huddled in blankets, they'd watch the babies struggle from the sand and make their run to the ocean.

Predators waited, ready to pounce on the hatchlings. The outer world could be a cruel place. Her mind flickered to Atlanta. If she'd known about the pain that waited for her there, would she still have gone?

The baby turtles didn't have a choice. They made it to the relative safety of the ocean or they perished. She had choices. So why did she so often seem to make the wrong one?

At last Miz Callie sank down next to her, face brimming with pleasure. "A fine nest, filled with eggs. Let's rest a moment, and then we can put tape up around it to keep the curious from getting too close."

"Your first nest of the season. That's reason to celebrate."

Miz Callie adjusted the brim of her sun hat and

linked her hands around her knees, smiling a little. "Reminds me of the very first time Mary Lyn and I found one. We couldn't have been more than six or seven."

This was the opening Georgia had hoped for. Now she had to figure out how to make the most of it. "Did Mary Lyn know Granddad's brother, too?"

"Land, yes, child. We all knew each other. Mary Lyn and Richmond and I were the same age, and we three did everything together." Her gaze softened, as if she looked back through time, seeing three bare-legged children running across the sand. "Ned was Richmond's big brother, you see. Such a kind boy. He always had time for us. Loved teaching us about the tides and the sea creatures, taking us shrimping with him. We purely adored him."

She patted her grandmother's hand. "I know you loved him. But that doesn't mean—"

"Sugar, I know all the arguments. I've had them in my head for months. That I saw him through a child's eyes. That I didn't know everything that happened. That even if he didn't want to fight, that didn't make him a coward."

"That's true, isn't it?" She said the words gently.

"I can't explain it," Miz Callie said. "All I can say is the more Mary Lyn and I talked about those days, the clearer that last summer came in my mind. I knew Ned, just about as well as Richmond did. He was brave and good. He couldn't suddenly turn around and become a coward. If he'd thought he couldn't fight, he'd have found another way to serve."

"Even so…" Even if her grandmother was right, it would be impossible to prove.

Miz Callie sighed. "I can't just leave it, child. I can't be like Mary Lyn, grieving for things left undone when she was dying." Her hand turned in Georgia's, so that she gripped it tightly. "I believe God led me to those memories for a reason, and it would be wrong to ignore that. You understand, don't you?"

She nodded. She understood that Miz Callie had a fierce need to do what she felt was right. She just hoped she hadn't chosen the wrong grandchild to help her.

Georgia's stomach fluttered as she and Miz Callie approached the Sullivan's Island playground that evening, and not with excitement over the dessert that awaited at the fire company's ice cream and cake social. She'd tried to beg off, but Miz Callie had looked at her as if she were crazy.

Miz Callie didn't understand. It was highly likely that some of her other relatives would show up tonight, casually seizing the opportunity to check in. The last thing she needed was questioning from her folks about her nonexistent progress in changing her grandmother's mind.

Or, for that matter, questions from her grandmother about Georgia's nonexistent progress on her quest.

The playground was filled with people—kids swarming over the swings and the slides, teenagers gathered in groups to self-consciously ignore their elders, grown-ups visiting with neighbors as they lined up for ice cream and cake.

"We may as well get right in line for dessert," Miz Callie said, chugging through the crowd with a firm grip on Georgia's arm. "I wonder if they've cut my cake yet."

Georgia had delivered her grandmother's delectable praline applesauce cake to the waiting refrigerated truck earlier in the afternoon. "It's probably gone already. You know how people love that cake."

Miz Callie flushed at the compliment even while brushing it off with a sweep of her hand. "There'll be plenty fancier than mine, I'm sure. Land, there's Marcy Dawson and her daughter. I haven't seen them in an age."

She veered off. Georgia followed, forcibly preventing herself from rolling her eyes like a disgruntled teenager. If you went anywhere in the greater Charleston area with Miz Callie, she'd be bound to find someone she knew.

The good thing about coming home was remembering how much she loved this place. The bad thing was a tendency to revert to a younger version of herself.

Marcy Dawson proved to be not a contemporary

of her grandmother's but someone more her mother's age, with windswept blond hair and perfectly tanned skin that was complemented by her white tennis shorts. Her daughter, with an apologetic smile, dashed off after an exploring toddler.

Ms. Dawson assessed Georgia with the air of someone fitting her into her proper niche. "You're Ashton and Delia's daughter, aren't you? I thought I heard you were working up in Atlanta, got yourself engaged, I believe your mother told me."

"I'm just back to visit for a bit." She slid her left hand behind her. "Helping my grandmother get settled at the cottage."

That distracted the woman, thank goodness, and she turned back to Miz Callie. "Is it true, then, that you're planning to stay on the island year-round?"

"That's right. My, word does get around. But then, you play bridge with my daughter-in-law, I believe." There was an icy edge to her grandmother's voice that Georgia didn't miss, maybe the faintest of suggestions that Georgia's mother had been talking out of turn.

"Well, I…" The woman looked around as if seeking escape. "I guess she might have mentioned something about it."

Miz Callie straightened, and Georgia caught her arm before she could say something Mamma and Daddy wouldn't appreciate.

"Miz Callie, we'd better get in line for our cake or we'll never get a table. Or better yet, why don't you find a table for us and save me a seat?"

Her grandmother sent her a look that said she knew exactly what Georgia was doing, but she allowed herself to be diverted. "I'll go find a scat, then. Mind you get me something chocolate now, y'heah?"

"I will." Miz Callie's passion for chocolate was second only to her love of the turtles. With a murmured good-bye to the Dawson woman, Georgia headed for the ticket booth.

Just her luck, to run into a bosom buddy of her mother's first thing. Not that she could keep her engagement-less status a secret for long, but Mamma had to hear about it from her, not from across the bridge table.

Deal with it, her conscience insisted, and she did her best to ignore that small voice.

Clutching the tickets, she headed for the long tables holding the cakes. A man stood, surveying the array, and an unwelcome tingle of awareness went through her. Matt.

She took a deep breath, pinned a smile to her face and stepped up to him. "What's wrong? Can't decide which one to choose?"

He turned and seemed genuinely pleased to see Georgia standing there. She felt her face flush with heat. "For someone who doesn't normally eat dessert, this is overwhelming. What do you recommend?"

"Well, first you eliminate all the ones you don't like and focus on what you do. Miz Callie has to have chocolate, the gooier the better, so I'm going for a slice of the double chocolate fudge cake for her."

"Decadent," he said, smiling as she put a slice on a paper plate. "What about you? Are you a chocolate addict like your grandmother?"

"I've always wanted to be like her," she admitted.

"Somehow I thought that might be true." His smile didn't slip, but his eyes were grave.

Maybe he understood that their special bond meant she had to protect her grandmother. And how was she going to do that when Miz Callie was headed straight for trouble?

"So, chocolate for you?" He held the server poised over the chocolate fudge.

"Actually, I think tonight I'll go with Miz Callie's praline applesauce cake." She slid the knife into the rich, moist layer. "She always wants to know that folks are eating what she baked."

"That's a sign of a loving heart, I've always heard—the need to feed people."

"She has that, all right." She hesitated, but no one was close enough to overhear them. "I just hope her loving heart won't lead her to a lot of pain."

"I know." His gaze warmed again as it rested on her face, and it was almost as if he touched her. "I don't want to see her hurt over this, either. I hope you can believe that."

"We both want the same thing, then," she said. "I just have to pray we can find some way to avoid disaster."

He stiffened. "If you're still thinking you can talk her out of this…"

"No." Her mind fled back to those moments on the dunes. "We talked about it. I understand why she's determined to go ahead. The only way we can prevent—"

"Georgia."

The voice behind her made her jump. She swung around, to be swept into a hug by her father.

"Mr. Harper," he said, with steel in his voice. "I see you've met my little girl."

Chapter Five

Matt nodded, not sure whether to offer his hand or not. Ashton Bodine hadn't been quite as outspoken as his brother on the subject of Matt's work for Miz Callie, but he'd certainly made his disapproval clear.

"Miz Callie introduced me to Georgia." It was on the tip of his tongue to add "…when she arrived," but he cut himself off. *Don't elaborate on your answers.* That's what he'd tell a client facing a hostile question, so maybe he'd better take his own advice.

Bodine's already erect figure straightened until he was almost standing at attention, his eyes as frosty as the touch of white in his hair. "I see."

Bodine could hardly control who his mother introduced to Matt, although it was clear that he'd like to. The silence stretched on awkwardly until someone moved between them, obviously impatient to reach the cake table.

Taking a step back, an excuse to leave already forming in his mind, he glanced at Georgia. And stopped. Georgia looked even more uncomfortable than he felt.

"You need a piece of cake for Lindsay." She rushed into speech, as if to deny that there was anything odd about this encounter. "What does she like?"

"Chocolate every time," he said, just as glad to turn away from Georgia's father.

Georgia snatched a piece of the double chocolate from the table. "What about you, Daddy? Aren't you having some cake?"

"I'll wait for your mother."

Georgia's tension level went up perceptibly at his words. She probably hated keeping Miz Callie's plans a secret from her parents, and he wasn't sure why she even bothered trying. It would all come out eventually.

Still, he couldn't claim he knew a thing about the complexities of families, since he'd had none to speak of. The series of foster homes he'd been in and out of hardly counted.

Jennifer had been his family, and then Lindsay.

"Well, I should take this to Miz Callie." She sounded relieved to have a reason to move.

"Not yet." Bodine's hand touched her elbow, staying her. "Here's your mamma now."

The woman who approached had Georgia's dark brown hair and brown eyes, but there the resemblance ended. While Georgia's hair dropped to her shoulders in unruly ringlets, her mother's was cut in a sleek, chin-length style. In contrast to her daughter's jeans and T-shirt, Mrs. Bodine wore silky white pants and a blouse, a sweater slung around her shoulders like a cape. She had the smooth elegance so many Southern women seemed born with.

Ignoring him, she touched her daughter's hair with a manicured fingernail. "Really, Georgia Lee." The soft drawl was gently chiding. "Let me make an appointment for you with my stylist while you're here. They must not know how to cut hair up there in Atlanta."

"It's fine, Mamma." Georgia pulled away, as she'd probably been doing since she was a teenager. "I didn't expect to see y'all here."

"We wouldn't miss the ice cream and cake social," her mother said, voice as silky as her blouse. "Come on, now, let's go find Miz Callie."

She turned away without even looking at him. As a cut, it was masterful.

"Mamma, have you met Miz Callie's attorney?" Georgia displayed unexpected steel. "This is Matthew Harper. Matt, my mother, Delia Bodine."

The woman shot Georgia an outraged stare before nodding coolly. "Mr. Harper. Now, what was it you're attending to for my mother-in-law?"

"I'm afraid I can't discuss a client's business," he said, careful to keep his tone pleasant. "Now, if you'll excuse me, I need to find my daughter."

Georgia meant well, he supposed, but there didn't seem to be any value in prolonging a conversation with her parents. Overcoming their antagonism was an impossible task.

He turned to scan the area, expecting to see Lindsay still on the swings. But she was sitting at a picnic table next to Miz Callie.

Suppressing a totally unreasonable surge of annoyance, he headed for them. He'd retrieve Lindsay, move to another table, and try to enjoy the evening without thinking about the inimical gazes directed at him.

As it turned out, Miz Callie had other ideas. She greeted him with a wide smile and a sweep of her hand to the bench.

"Come, sit down. We've been saving a place for you."

"I think Lindsay and I should find a table of our own, since your son and his wife are joining you." He rested his hand on Lindsay's shoulder.

She pulled away, shaking her head. "Miz Callie said we could sit with her."

"That's right." She waved to the Bodines, gesturing to the benches. "Come on, everyone sit down. Lindsay and I picked the best table here in the shade."

Short of being rude, there was nothing he could do.

Apparently Georgia's parents felt the same, and in a moment they were all seated around the picnic table.

Spanish moss, drifting in the breeze, made moving shadows on Georgia's face as she leaned over to hand out cups of ice cream. When she slid one to Lindsay, his daughter shoved it away.

"I don't want chocolate."

"Lindsay, that's your favorite." Her comment was impolite, but he didn't want to scold her in front of other people.

Her lips tightened for a moment. Then she took the ice cream. "Thank you," she muttered.

Miz Callie diverted attention with a comment about the turnout, Georgia's father responded and the talk became general.

Matt glanced at his child under cover of the conversation. Lindsay was snuggled close to Miz Callie, almost deliberately ignoring the others.

What was that all about? That too-familiar helpless feeling rolled over him. Jennifer had been the one to handle everything where their daughter was concerned, and he'd been so busy getting his career going that he'd let her. Even then, he'd sometimes felt a little envious of their close bond. Now...now too often he felt adrift, ill-prepared for the role he had to fill.

Georgia sat next to her father, her face relaxing when he said something in a low, relaxing tone. For just an instant he envied their closeness.

"Georgia's always been her daddy's girl," Miz

Callie said softly. "She missed him terribly when he had to be away."

"Away?"

"Ashton was in the Coast Guard for thirty years. The boys missed him, too, of course, but it affected Georgia the most."

So the Bodines were a military family. That went a long way toward explaining Miz Callie's reluctance to confide in them about her plans.

"Tell me, Mr. Harper. Where were you raised?" Delia Bodine's question, cutting across the table, startled him.

"Boston," he said. And not raised so much as thrown out to strive or fail on his own. "I lived there all my life until we moved down here."

"Let me think." She gazed at her husband. "Ashton, do we know anybody in Boston?"

"There was that Carlton boy who was in Cole's year at the Citadel. He was from Boston."

"Margo Lawton's daughter married someone from Boston, I believe," Delia said. "Or Cambridge, maybe. Now, what was his name?"

He recognized what was going on. His partner had explained to him the particularly Southern passion that could be encapsulated in one question. *Who are your family?* They wanted to place people.

Well, they wouldn't place him, no matter how they tried.

"Cambridge is near Boston, isn't it?" Delia fixed

a cool stare on him. "Was your home anywhere close?"

"More cake, Miz Callie?" Georgia reached for her grandmother's plate.

Delia broke off her questioning to stare at her daughter's hand, gasping a little. "Georgia! Your ring! Don't tell me you've lost it. What on earth will James say?"

Georgia snatched her hand back as if she could hide the evidence. "I didn't lose it, Mamma."

"Well, then, where is it?"

Delia had forgotten about him. The relief he felt was tempered with regret that his reprieve had come at Georgia's expense.

Georgia put down the plate she was holding. "I gave it back to James. The engagement is off."

How much it cost her to say that bluntly in front of all of them, he couldn't imagine.

"What do you mean?" Delia Bodine looked as horrified as if her daughter had announced that she was taking up bank robbery. "How could you—"

"Enough, Delia." Georgia's father didn't raise his voice, but it held a tone of command. "We can talk about this later. I'm sure Georgia had a good reason for her decision."

Georgia's eyes sparkled with unshed tears. "Thank you, Daddy."

He'd like to say something comforting, but it wasn't his place. Maybe the best thing he could do for her was make himself scarce, so the Bodine family could have this out in private.

"About done, Lindsay?" He slid off the bench. "I think we should head for home."

"I don't want to go yet," Lindsay wailed. "It's not late. Why do we have to go?"

He resisted the urge to explain and held out his hand to his daughter. "It's time."

For an instant he thought she'd argue. Then, pouting, she slid off the bench.

"Say good-night to everyone," he prompted.

"Good night," she mumbled, gaze on her feet.

He was conscious of Delia's critical eye on his child, and irritation flared. She had no right to criticize. Currently, she wasn't doing such a great job with her own daughter.

Georgia leaned against her father, and Ashton Bodine put his arm around her.

Matt said good-night, wondering whether he'd ever have that kind of closeness with his child.

Georgia stretched, cracking one eye open to glare at the sunlight streaming through the bedroom window. She always put the shade up when she slept in this bedroom so that she could see the stars when she fell asleep and be awakened by the sunlight on the waves. But today she could have easily pulled the covers back over her head.

Instead, she swung her feet to the floor, toes

curling into the rag rug that covered the bare boards. Normally she slept soundly, but last night her dreams had been a confused kaleidoscope of people and images. She couldn't remember specifics, but she'd woken with her throat clogged with unshed tears.

Because of James? Maybe so.

She stretched, trying to shake off the feeling, but it persisted, even while she pulled on shorts and a T-shirt and drew her hair into a ponytail.

James had shown he wasn't the man she'd thought he was—the man she'd fallen in love with. She'd been right to break it off, no matter what anyone said—anyone, in this case, being her mother. She'd tried to explain, hampered by the fact that she didn't want to tell them she'd lost her job as well as her fiancé. There'd be time enough for that revelation when she'd decided what she was going to do with herself.

And in the meantime, there was Miz Callie's problem to focus on. She shoved her feet into sneakers and headed for the stairs.

No sign of Miz Callie until she glanced through the sliding glass doors. Her grandmother was on the deck, red plastic bucket in hand, saying something to Lindsay, who looked up at her with an adoring expression.

Grabbing an apple from the pewter bowl on the table, she hurried out to join them.

"Hi. Wow, it's going to be a hot one."

Miz Callie settled her floppy hat on her head. "That's why Lindsay and I are going on turtle patrol so early."

"You like the turtles, too?" She smiled at Lindsay.

The child nodded, but her gaze slid away from Georgia's.

"Come along," Miz Callie said. "You may as well get some exercise with us, since you slept right through your runnin' time."

"I did, didn't I?" She stretched again, stifling a yawn, and nodded. "Okay, let's go."

Miz Callie handed her the bucket, filled with the paraphernalia they'd need if they found a new nest.

Lindsay's lower lip came out in a pout. "You said I could carry it. That's not fair."

Georgia gave the bucket to the child. "Sure thing, Lindsay."

Lindsay snatched the bucket and spun to hurry down the stairs. A reluctant "thanks" floated back.

Georgia looked at her grandmother as they followed her. Miz Callie shrugged and shook her head in a not-in-front-of-the-child way.

When they reached the packed sand where the walking was easier, Lindsay danced along the lacy ripples of incoming waves.

Miz Callie smiled. "You used to do that very thing."

"All kids do, don't they? Well, maybe the boys didn't. They always had some plan to carry out."

"Mischief, as often as not." Miz Callie was smiling.

Lindsay's small figure looked as light and insubstantial as one of the sandpipers when she spun, her hair swinging in a pale arc.

"She doesn't like me, does she?"

"I wouldn't say that." Miz Callie shook her head, sighing a little. "Truth is, she's probably a bit jealous. You coming along, snagging my attention. And her father's."

"I haven't—" She gulped. "I haven't snagged Matt's attention, as you so elegantly put it. I'm only spending time with him because you got me into this."

"Lindsay doesn't know that." Her grandmother watched the child, frowning. "She's just desperate for folks to make her feel safe in this new place, with her mother gone and all. She's a bit lost."

Georgia winced. She'd felt that way herself.

"I should let her have her walk with you." She stopped. "I could make some excuse…"

Miz Callie linked her arm in Georgia's. "You'll do no such thing. Might be good for that child to see that family can be bigger than just a couple of people."

"She and Matt do seem pretty much on their own. Has he ever mentioned any other family to you?"

"I can't say he has." She sent Georgia a shadowed glance. "Speaking of family, I got together the information Matt asked for. I'll show you when we get back to the house."

Georgia blinked. "What did you do—stay up all night looking for things?"

"Most of it was right there in your grandfather's family Bible. The rest—well, I guess I did sit up a mite late. When you're my age, you don't need as much sleep as you used to."

"Even so—" She stopped, because Miz Callie was clearly not listening.

Instead, her grandmother was staring landward with a look of outrage on her face. Before Georgia could react, Miz Callie went striding toward the dunes, waving her hat.

"What do you think you're doing? Get away from that!"

Georgia ran to catch up as Miz Callie approached the people on the dunes. Tourists, she could see at a glance. A sunburned man with a kid in tow. The boy had crawled under the plastic tape that marked off the turtle's nest and was burrowing in the sand.

"Stop it, you hear me?"

The boy kept right on with what he was doing, and the man shot her an annoyed glance. "The kid's not doing any harm, lady. He just wants to see the turtle eggs."

"Get him out of there." Miz Callie glared at him. "This is a protected area. As the tape clearly shows."

"Hey, we're just trying to see a little nature.

Something for him to talk about when he gets home."

Miz Callie, apparently too impatient to argue, shoved past the man and tapped the boy. "Out!"

"Ow! Leave me alone!" The boy, as ill-mannered as his father, swung his shovel at Miz Callie's arm.

Her grandmother winced as it landed with a thwack. Georgia stepped over the tape, grasped the boy's arms and pulled him away from the hole he'd made, avoiding the kick he aimed at her shins.

"It is a federal crime to interfere with the sea turtles," she said loudly, drowning out the kid's yells and the father's protests. "If you're not out of here in two minutes, I'm calling the police."

That silenced them. The man grabbed his son and pulled him away. With a fulminating glance, he stalked off, the boy wailing his desire to dig up the turtle's nest.

Georgia took a deep breath and turned to her grandmother. "Are you all right?"

"I'm fine, darlin'. Just fine." She smoothed her hand along her wrist. "The little monster just landed a hit on my bad wrist, that's all. But you…" She looked at Georgia with the beginnings of a smile in her eyes. "Child, you purely tore a strip off them. I didn't know you had it in you to lose your temper like that."

Georgia gave a shaky laugh. "I didn't, either. I guess when I saw him hit you—"

"He was a bad kid." The small voice came from behind them. They'd forgotten Lindsay in the excitement.

Her grandmother reached for the child and pulled her close in a comforting hug. "Let's just say he's been badly brought up. No one has taught him to observe the rules."

Lindsay put her arm around Miz Callie's waist, as if to assure herself that she was all right. "He didn't understand about the turtles, did he?"

Georgia grinned. "I see you've indoctrinated her already."

"Of course." She hugged Lindsay. "I'm fine, child. He'll think twice before he bothers a nest again."

"Georgia sure told him." Lindsay's solemn gaze rested on her, a little more favorably.

"Well, I tried." She got down on her knees and crawled under the tape. "Want to help me fix the nest?"

Nodding, Lindsay crawled in next to her and imitated Georgia's movements, filling in the hole and smoothing sand over it.

When they'd finished, they crawled back out again and stood to survey their handiwork.

"Good job." She rested her hands on her hips. "Looks just like it should, don't you think?"

Lindsay put her own small hands on her hips. "Yes, I do," she said definitely.

Georgia suppressed a smile. Maybe Lindsay's quarrel with her had been overcome.

That seemed borne out as they started back down the beach. Lindsay skipped along between them.

"Did you used to look for turtle nests with your grandmother when you were little?" she asked, tilting her face up toward Georgia.

"I sure did. Miz Callie taught me and my brothers everything I know about the ocean and the shore."

"How many brothers do you have?"

"Two. Both older than me. And a whole mess of cousins. When we were all here together, we made quite a tribe." She smiled at the memory. They were all close enough in age that they'd played and fought as equals.

"I wish I had cousins. Or brothers." Lindsay's voice sounded very small.

Georgia exchanged a concerned glance with her grandmother over the child's head. "Maybe you'll get some cousins. If your aunt or uncle gets married, then their children would be your cousins."

"I don't have any aunts or uncles. Just Daddy. And my grandparents. They live in Arizona."

It sounded lonely. She tried to imagine what her life would have been like without her big, sprawling, noisy, interfering family. She couldn't.

"Tell you what," she said, putting her hand lightly on Lindsay's shoulder. "Next time we all get together, you can be a part of our tribe. Okay?"

Lindsay stared up at her as if measuring the sincerity of her words. Finally she gave a quick little nod.

"Okay," she said. She sighed, a very grown-up sound. "I have to go. I'm going to Bible school this morning."

"That'll be fun," Miz Callie said. "You come by later and tell us all about it, okay?"

"Okay." Lindsay looked a little brighter. "I'll see you later." She trudged off toward her house.

Georgia stood and watched her until she reached the deck. "I see what you mean. Poor kid. She's lonely."

"Hopefully she'll make some friends at Bible school." Miz Callie put her arm around Georgia's waist as they headed to the house.

"Did you arrange that?"

"I might have suggested it," her grandmother admitted. "Let's get something to eat, and you can go over my notes. And I thought, since you're going to have lunch downtown, you might drop them off at Matt's office so he can get going right away."

"How did you hear about my lunch date?" She lifted an eyebrow at Miz Callie as they walked up the stairs. She didn't think her grandmother had been around when her cousin Amanda had called with an invitation to meet for lunch.

Miz Callie chuckled. "Child, if you want to keep secrets, don't belong to such a nosy family. I just happened to be talking to your brother, and he mentioned that Lucas mentioned it to him."

Lucas was Amanda's big brother and just as inclined to butt into everyone else's business as the rest of them.

Her thoughts drifted to Matt and Lindsay, alone and isolated. All in all, she guessed she'd take the family she had, annoying as they could be.

Chapter Six

"Mr. Harper?" Madie Dillon, the secretary Matt shared with Rodney Porter, tapped and opened his office door a few inches. "You have a visitor. Shall I ask her to make an appointment?"

Visitors were so unusual that for a moment he couldn't think how to answer. "Who is it?"

"Georgia Bodine." Madie seemed surprised, too. Clients hadn't exactly been beating down his door.

"Show her in." He rose, buttoning the top button of his shirt and tightening his tie.

There she was, the door closing behind her. Instead of her usual shorts and T-shirt, she wore a turquoise sundress that swirled around her slim body and emphasized her tan legs.

"I'm so sorry if I'm disturbing you." She sent a quick, curious glance around the office. "Miz Callie insisted I stop by."

"Not a problem." He rounded the desk and drew one of the comfortable leather chairs around for her. "Please sit down."

She slid onto the chair. "Nice."

"Nothing but the best for Rodney Porter's clients." He took the other chair and sat facing her.

She lifted an eyebrow. "And Matthew Harper's clients, too?"

"I'm a very small cog in the wheel right now," he said. He swung his hand in a gesture that encompassed the whole office. "I feel like a fraud sometimes, sitting in the midst of all this Southern elegance. This was Rod's brother-in-law's office, before he ran off with his secretary."

"I remember. That news traveled all the way to Atlanta. So Rodney brought you in to replace him."

"Not exactly." He felt compelled to be more open with her than he'd been with most people he'd met here. "Rod was being a friend. He knew I wanted to leave Boston for a fresh start after Jennifer's death, and he made it possible."

Georgia's gaze lit on something on his desk. Without turning, he felt quite sure it was the silver-framed photo of Jennifer.

"Is that Jennifer?"

Nodding, he lifted the frame and handed it to her. "That was taken on our honeymoon."

Jennifer sat on a rock in the black-and-white photo, staring out at a foggy sea. The wind whipped her hair around her face, and her hands were clasped around her knees. They'd gone up the Maine coast, dawdling in one small town after another, with no set destination and no timetable to keep.

"She was very beautiful." Georgia stared at the image for a moment longer, as if it would tell her something about him. Then she handed it back. "Thank you for letting me see it. Lindsay's like her, isn't she?"

He nodded, throat tightening. Most of the time he ignored the resemblance, but sometimes a turn of the head or a quick, light movement brought hot tears to his eyes.

He cleared his throat. "What can I do for Miz Callie today?"

Georgia bent to pick up a folder she'd placed on the floor next to her handbag. "These are the notes she came up with last night—names, dates, addresses." She handed him the folder.

He flipped it open, then leaned over so she could see it, too. As she'd said, names and addresses, birth dates, death dates, all in Miz Callie's fine, spidery writing.

"Is this information you'd be familiar with?"

She traced a fingertip down the page. "Pretty much, although I'd never have come up with the dates." She pointed to an address on King Street in Charleston. "That's the house Miz Callie lived in before she got the idea to move out to the island full-time. I guess Granddad inherited it from his parents after Ned…" She paused. "After Ned left. Or died." Her gaze met his. "I mean, he was older than my grandfather by several years, so he's probably dead by now, don't you think?"

"Hard to say. You'd think, if he were alive, he'd have gotten in touch with the family sometime in all these years."

She shrugged, frowning. "True. But if he died, you'd think the family would have been notified."

"Maybe, maybe not. It depends on the circumstances and how well he'd created a new life."

Her frown deepened. "It's not impossible, is it? To find the answers my grandmother wants?"

"Not impossible." He wouldn't sugarcoat it for her. "But it may be very difficult. And even if we find the answers, they may not make her happy."

Georgia sighed deeply, running a hand through her hair.

He smiled. "I understand the frustration, believe me. It's not the first time a client has insisted on doing something I advised against."

"At least you're not going up against the rest of the family, too."

"I wouldn't count on that. I've already had visits from your father and your uncle."

"I'm sorry about that."

She looked so distressed that he nearly laughed.

"Don't worry, Georgia. Your father was the soul of politeness."

"He would be. Not Uncle Brett, though, I'll bet. It was Brett, wasn't it, and not Harrison?"

"Yes. Do I have another one to look forward to?"

"I hope not." She seemed relieved by his light tone. "They just want to protect Miz Callie, you know."

"I know. It's good that she has so many relatives who care about her. Sometimes elderly people don't."

"There are lots of us, that's for sure." She sounded as if she thought it a mixed blessing. "Lindsay was telling us about her grandparents this morning. That they live clear out in Arizona, so she doesn't see them very often. Are they your folks?"

"Jennifer's parents. My father-in-law's health isn't great, and he seems to do better out there."

"It's a shame they're so far away. And your parents?"

"Dead." At least, he supposed they were. They were certainly dead to him.

"I'm sorry." Sympathy filled her eyes, turning them that deep, velvety brown. "It must be rough, being so alone."

He shrugged. "I'm used to it." If he kept on looking into those eyes, he'd lean so far forward that he'd be in danger of falling off his chair.

He busied himself shuffling through the few papers in the folder. He'd felt the attraction last night, when he'd held her hand so briefly. Felt it again now.

But that was all it was. He'd already had the big love of his life. He wasn't foolish enough to think he could replace that.

"I'll put in some time on the search this afternoon." He closed the folder and put it on his desk. "I'm sorry Miz Callie sent you into town on such a hot day. I'm sure you'd rather be on the beach."

"I was coming anyway. I'm meeting my cousin Amanda for lunch." She glanced at her watch, a slim gold bracelet on her tanned wrist. "And I'm late."

He stood when she did and followed her toward the door. "Thanks again."

She turned so suddenly that he nearly bumped into her. "I just—I wanted to thank you. I don't suppose Miz Callie realizes it, but I know you're taking valuable time away from your other business in order to do this."

She was so close he could almost count the freckles the sun had spattered on her nose. "Don't worry about it. I'm not exactly overwhelmed with business, believe me."

"I see." She gave him a wry smile. "Not easy for an outsider to break in, is it? Folks around here tend to be a little clannish."

"I've noticed." He was so distracted by Georgia's

proximity, he hardly knew what he was saying. "I'll hang in. It's too important to me not to. Just one good case could make all the difference."

She stiffened, taking a step backward.

"I guess Miz Callie is that big case, isn't she?" Her eyes were accusing him of something.

He clamped his lips for a moment before answering. "If Miz Callie is pleased with my services, naturally I hope she'll mention me to people. Word of mouth really is the best advertising."

"Yes, of course." Her voice was cold as she reached behind her for the doorknob. "I hope it works out for you."

Before he could come up with something else to say, she'd slipped out the door.

Georgia parked carefully in the restaurant's minuscule parking lot, holding her breath as she slipped between two oversized SUVs. Parking space in Charleston was at a premium. A city built centuries ago on a peninsula was bound to have that issue.

She walked toward the restaurant that backed onto the water. It was new since the last time she'd been here, occupying a building that had once belonged to the navy.

The breeze off the water cooled her overheated face but not her disposition.

Matt hadn't even realized he'd upset her. She was just part of the job. And Miz Callie was a way of making inroads into the tight mesh that was Charleston society.

What else had she expected? She'd seen enough workaholic males in her time. She just hadn't recognized it quite soon enough in Matt.

A wall of cool air and the scent of frying hush puppies greeted her when she pushed through the door. Before the hostess could speak to her, Georgia spotted her cousin sitting at the far end of the room in front of the windows. With a quick wave, Georgia wove her way between the tables to reach her.

"Georgia Lee, it is mighty good to see you." Amanda surged from the chair to wrap her arms around her. "It's been way too long. Let me look at you." She gave her a critical stare. "Well, I don't see it."

"See what?"

"Your mother told my mother you looked like you'd been dragged through a knothole backwards." She grinned. "But you look pretty good to me."

"You know my mother. She's only pleased if I'm dressed for the cotillion."

She slid into the seat opposite Amanda, looking at her cousin with pleasure. Amanda's sleek brown hair dropped to her shoulders, her green eyes sparkled in a lightly tanned face and she had the polished look down to an art. Come to think of it, Mamma probably wondered why her daughter couldn't be more like Cousin Amanda.

"Mothers." Amanda dismissed them with a wave of a well-manicured hand. "Tell the truth now. Miz Callie's been spoiling you since you got back, now hasn't she?"

"Just like always," she said lightly. She'd love to tell Amanda what was going on with their grandmother and have the benefit of Amanda's shrewd advice. With her nimble brain and deep interest in people, Amanda seemed born for her job on the daily newspaper.

But she couldn't tell. It wasn't her secret to share.

"I got you a sweet tea." Amanda shoved the glass toward her, ice tinkling with the movement. "And I went ahead and ordered our shrimp salads, so we could get on with lunch. Some of us aren't on vacation, you know."

"I'm sure your boss will have you drawn and quartered if you're not back in time." She took a sip of the tea.

"He might." Amanda scowled at the table. She'd been complaining about her boss the last time they'd talked, and apparently things were no better.

"How is work going? You getting to cover anything bigger than the latest oyster roast?"

"I'll have you know I graduated to the dog show last week." Amanda grinned, affection flowing easily between them.

Cousins were special, Miz Callie had always reminded them when they fought, and she'd been right. The bonds she'd formed early with her cousins were nearly as strong as those with her brothers. And at least some of the cousins were girls.

"How's Annabel?" Amanda's twin sister looked like her, but the resemblance was strictly on the surface. In every other way, they were polar opposites.

Amanda made a face. "Still running that horse farm over on James Island. Go see her—she'd love it. But don't wear your good shoes."

"That sounds like the voice of experience talking."

"Believe me, it is." Amanda's eyes grew solemn suddenly, and she reached out to grasp Georgia's hand. "Enough chitchat. What's this about your engagement being over, sugar? You catch him with another girl?"

"Not quite. I take it the news is all over the family already." Not that she'd expected anything else.

"Honey, it's probably all over Charleston. You know how the family is."

"I know, believe me, I know."

"So what's the scoop? Now, don't tell me if you don't want to, but you know I'm dying to hear."

She hesitated, but the cat was already out of the bag. Amanda might sound acerbic, but underneath was a strong vein of empathy, and the urge to spill the story was strong. "Take my advice and never get engaged to someone you work with. It makes for messy loyalties. I thought we were partners, you know? Then I found out he was taking my work and presenting it as his own. He even had the nerve to think I should be pleased about that."

Amanda squeezed her hand. "He was a jerk. A charming jerk. You take my advice and never get involved with a charmer. You're well rid of him."

She managed a smile. "Unfortunately I'm rid of a job, as well. He managed to blame his mistakes on me, and I got the axe."

Amanda's eyes sparked with outrage. "Didn't you fight back? Go to his boss?"

"I just wanted to get away and forget the whole thing."

"Honey…"

The waitress appeared with their salads, and Georgia leaned back while she put them on the table along with a basket of hush puppies. Beyond the window, boats moved busily in and out of Charleston harbor pleasure boats, container ships from who-knew-where, a tour boat on its way to Fort Sumter. The gulls wheeled and shrieked, a back ground so familiar that she almost didn't hear it any longer.

When the woman moved away, she shook her head at Amanda. "Don't bother to give me the pep talk. You'd fight back. But I'm not like you. Listen, just forget about it, okay? I'm moving on."

"If you say so. Anyway, you know I'm on your

side, every time." Amanda speared her fork into a mound of shrimp salad. "If we're not going to talk about your engagement, I guess we'd better fall back on Miz Callie. Sorry you got landed with trying to change her mind, but that's what happens when you're the favorite granddaughter."

"Get out. You know very well Miz Callie doesn't play favorites."

"Maybe not." Amanda tapped her pink nail on her glass. "But I'm glad I'm not the one trying to convince her."

"You know, and I know, that trying to convince Miz Callie to stop doing something she wants to do is…is…"

"…like trying to stop the tide," Amanda finished for her. "Why do you s'pose our folks don't see that?"

"I can't imagine." Her life would be so much easier if they did.

Amanda glanced at her wristwatch. "You talk. I've got to eat so I can get back to the newspaper."

The newspaper. In her job, Amanda would have ready access to the papers from the time they were interested in.

Did she really want to bring Amanda in on this? She hesitated, eying her cousin.

"Whatever it is, you might as well just spit it out." Amanda's eyebrows lifted. "Come on, Georgia Lee. I know when you're chewing on something."

"What elegant phrasing. You use that in the paper?"

"Out with it. You want something. I can tell."

She hesitated, studying her cousin's face. "Could you look up something in the newspaper files for me without asking questions or mentioning it to anyone else?"

Amanda tilted her head slightly. "Even family?"

"Especially family."

Her smile curved. "I promise. Cousins' honor." She made a quick gesture, crossing her heart.

Georgia took a breath and prayed she was doing the right thing. "Will you check the papers for the summer of 1942 and see if you can find anything about Edward Bodine?"

For a moment Amanda's green eyes simply looked puzzled. Then Georgia saw recognition dawn.

"Edward Bodine. Granddad's brother? The one who…" She didn't finish the sentence.

"Uncle Ned. Right." She grasped Amanda's hand. "Say no if you want to. Just don't tell anyone."

Amanda studied her for a long moment. Then she grinned. "When did I ever say no to trouble? I'll do my best. But I wish I knew what you're up to."

Relief swept through her. She could count on Amanda. "You're better off not knowing."

"Okay. I'll buy that." Amanda stared at her for a long moment. "But just remember one thing, Georgia Lee. People who play with fire are likely to get burned."

Chapter Seven

Georgia had hoped to get her grandmother reminiscing about Uncle Ned that evening, but once they'd finished the dishes, she found that Lindsay was joining them. Something in her expression must have alerted Miz Callie that she wasn't thrilled at the thought.

"I enjoy having Lindsay here," Miz Callie said, emphasizing the words with the clatter of a pot lid into the sink. "Is that a problem for you?"

Her disenchantment with Matt couldn't be allowed to affect her attitude toward the little girl. "I'm glad to see Lindsay. I was looking forward to having a nice talk with my favorite grandmother, that's all."

Miz Callie waved the words away with a flip of her dish towel, smiling. "She won't stay long, so we can talk all you want later. Matt has to finish up some work at the office after supper."

It was probably the work he'd neglected while he was searching through tedious computer records for Ned Bodine. She ought to feel grateful. She would, if she didn't understand his motives so clearly.

"Here she comes now." Miz Callie peered out the kitchen window. "We're goin' on the beach. You coming?"

"I'll be along in a minute. I want to get something."

When she descended the stairs a few minutes later, Miz Callie was ensconced in her favorite beach chair, with Lindsay digging in the sand at her feet.

Grabbing a chair, Georgia slung the cloth bag containing her sketching materials over her shoulder. She walked down the short path through the dunes.

"Hey." She flipped the beach chair open and sat down. "You diggin' your way to China, Lindsay?"

"I'm making a lake for Julie and Janie to play in." Julie and Janie were apparently the two tiny plastic dolls that lay on the sand.

"They'll like that." She opened the sketch pad and sat back, taking in the scene.

The tide ebbed, leaving an expanse of shining sand traced with an intricate pattern of ghost crab trails and sandpiper prints. She began to draw.

Lindsay appeared at her elbow. "What are you drawing?"

"What I see." That probably sounded a little short, though she didn't mean it that way. "I have an extra pad with me. Would you like to draw?"

Lindsay clasped her hands behind her back. "I'm not very good."

It was the sort of thing she said about herself. She didn't like hearing it from Lindsay. "Drawing is one of those things you can do just for fun." She held the pad and a few colored pencils out to Lindsay.

"What should I draw?" She sat on the sand.

"What do you see?"

Lindsay craned her neck as she looked around. "I see a sea gull sitting in the sand. But that'd be hard to draw."

"For fun, remember?"

Lindsay nodded. Then she bent over the pad.

Georgia tried to concentrate on her own drawing, but she couldn't help watching Lindsay. The child was certainly tied up in knots. Was that part of the aftermath of losing her mother? She couldn't even guess.

She'd never thought herself particularly maternal. Annabel, Amanda's twin, had all the maternal instincts. Even when they were children, it was always Annabel who comforted people and critters when they hurt. She'd collected more strays than the animal shelter.

She didn't have those instincts, but she felt the softening of her heart when she watched Lindsay. Despite a large, loving family, she knew what it was to feel lonely.

Lindsay held the pad back a little, frowning at her picture. "It doesn't look right. See?"

True, the picture didn't look much like the sea gull, but at least it was identifiable as a bird.

"I like it," she said. "I don't believe I drew birds that well when I was seven." She handed it to her grandmother.

"I do like it, too. I'll bet you'd enjoy coloring it, wouldn't you?"

"Yes, ma'am."

That was the first time she'd heard Lindsay add the familiar Southern grace note of calling Miz Callie "ma'am," and it made both of them smile.

"You're turning into a real island girl," Miz Callie said. "Even sounding like a native."

Lindsay frowned. "What's a native?"

"Somebody who was born here, sugar." Georgia tugged the blond ponytail lightly. "But we take outlanders, too, long as they learn as fast as you do."

Lindsay bent over her picture, but Georgia didn't miss the smile that tugged at the corner of her mouth.

Lindsay shot a sideways glance at Georgia. "You said I was seven. But I'm almost eight."

"It's a good picture, even for an eight-year-old," Georgia said promptly.

"Almost eight." Miz Callie echoed the child's words. "When is your birthday?"

"Tuesday." A cloud crossed Lindsay's face. "Last

year I had a party at the jump palace with all my friends. My mommy got me a cake with a princess on it."

They were silent for a moment.

"I'll bet your daddy is planning to do something special." *He'd better be.*

She shrugged. "He said maybe I could have a party. But I don't know enough kids to invite to a party."

"You know me," Miz Callie said briskly. "And you know Georgia, and I'll bet you're meeting some friends at Bible school."

"That's right." At this point, she'd say just about anything to wipe that woebegone look from Lindsay's face. "You'll have a real island celebration for your birthday."

"What's this about a birthday?" Matt's voice sounded behind them.

Georgia jerked around. She'd expected to see him walking down the beach, at which point she could have disappeared into the house. He'd evidently parked in front of Miz Callie's and come back on the path instead.

"We were talking about Lindsay's birthday," Miz Callie said, getting up and stretching. "We can't believe she's going to be eight already."

"Next week." Matt leaned over Lindsay's chair. "What a great picture. Did Georgia help you?"

"She did it all herself," Georgia said quickly.

"Georgia let me use her paper and pencils," Lindsay said. "I want to give it to Miz Callie."

"Why, thank you so much." Miz Callie held out her arm, and Lindsay went to lean against her. "We'll hang it up in the kitchen so I can see it every day."

Miz Callie's refrigerator had always been host to a rotating display of grandkids' art. Now Lindsay's picture would take its place there.

Lindsay glanced at her father. "Can I help hang it up before we go home?"

"Sure enough." Miz Callie started to pick up her chair, but Matt took it from her.

"You go ahead. I'll help Georgia take the chairs up."

Obviously he had something to say to her. Miz Callie held out her hand to Lindsay. "We'll see if there are any cookies in the jar, long as we're going to the kitchen."

Georgia watched them head for the cottage, her throat tightening. Her grandmother had become a little stooped, moving more slowly than she once did. But she still focused her total attention on the child by her side.

She bent to pick up a chair, but Matt stopped her.

"Wait. Please." The *please* sounded like an after-thought. "We need to talk."

"I have to go in." She didn't want to hear anything he had to say, not right at the moment. Maybe they had to work together, but she wouldn't let herself be drawn into believing this was anything more than business to him.

"It's important."

Her gaze rose to his face. "Did you find out something?"

"No, I didn't. Why are you angry with me?"

The blunt question shook her. She looked away, refusing to meet his eyes. "Why would I be angry?" Her voice sounded calm and detached, and she was proud of that.

"That's what I'd like to know." His fingers closed on her hand, as if to keep her there, and his palm was warm against her skin. "One minute we were talking about your grandmother's case, and the next you shot out of my office as if a monster were after you."

"I didn't…I mean, I was late." Why didn't she just tell him? Amanda would. Amanda would square up to him and tell him just what she thought.

But she wasn't Amanda.

"That's not it, and you know it." His voice was edged with frustration, and his fingers pressed against her skin. "Tell me what's wrong."

Her heart began to thud. "You! You're what's wrong."

He stared at her blankly. "What are you talking about?" His eyes grew icy. "I'm an outsider, is that it?"

"No, that's not it. I don't care where you're from. I do care that you're using my grandmother to further your career."

He stiffened. "Is that really what you think of me?"

"That's what you said. You need a big case involving someone who'll give you the opening you need to break in here. My grandmother was perfect for you, wasn't she? Everybody knows the Bodine name. You took advantage of living next door to her. You talked her into—"

"Stop right there." The words were so heavy with anger that they silenced her.

But he didn't continue. Instead he took a breath, looked down at his hand gripping hers and loosened his hold so that his fingers encircled her wrist lightly.

"Let's back up. All right, yes, I did say that I needed a client of my own." His eyes darkened with pain. "I'm not going to apologize for wanting to succeed here. I have Lindsay to consider."

His voice roughened, twisting her heart against her will.

"My daughter doesn't have anybody else. I took a chance, moving here. I have to make it work."

She didn't want to sympathize. Didn't want to understand. "My grandmother—"

"Miz Callie came to me." He said the words evenly, as if to give equal weight to each of them.

"Georgia, I did not try to convince her to do this. She had already decided exactly what she wanted. She laid it all out for me." His lips twisted in a wry smile. "Do you really think I could talk her into anything she didn't want to do?"

"No." Her voice was small when she admitted it. "I guess not. But I thought you were doing this because you wanted to help her. Because you liked her. Not because you thought her influence would establish you here."

"I do like her. How could I help it? Her kindness to Lindsay is enough to put me in her debt."

The passion in his voice moved her. "Even so…"

"Even so, I hope doing this job for her will bring me new clients. But from what you've said, it might have exactly the opposite effect."

She hadn't thought of that. She'd jumped to conclusions about his motives without thinking it through, maybe because she'd had enough of men who'd sacrifice anything or anyone for the sake of success. Shame colored her cheeks.

"I hope that won't happen. For all of our sakes. I'm sorry, Matt. I reacted without thinking." Her cheeks were hot, and she had to force herself to meet his eyes.

He didn't speak for a minute, though he looked as if words hovered on his tongue. With his hand closed around her wrist, he must feel the way her pulse was racing.

"It's okay," he said finally, and she had the feeling that wasn't what he'd intended to say. "I hope that, too, but either way, I'm in this to the finish. No matter what happens."

She nodded, her throat too tight to speak.

He held her hand for a moment longer. Then he let it go slowly, maybe reluctantly. He picked up the chairs.

"We'd better go in."

As she followed him toward the house, she knew that something had changed between them again, like the sand shifting under her feet when she stood in the waves on the ebbing tide. She knew how to keep her balance in the surf. But this change—she didn't know whether to be excited or afraid or both.

Window panes rattled as the wind whipped around the beach house. Georgia leaned against the sliding glass door, shielding her eyes with her hand as she peered out into the dark.

"It sounds as if there's rain coming." She couldn't see much, but she recognized the signs.

"A line of thunderstorms is coming through, according to the weather." Miz Callie looked up from the newspaper she was reading, "I already drew some water and got the candles out, just in case it gets bad."

Miz Callie believed in being prepared, like most of the old-timers. The island had seen its share of bad weather over the years.

Thunder boomed overhead, and her grandmother put the paper aside. "I'll get the candles…"

"I'll do it."

Georgia waved her back to her padded rocking chair and hurried into the kitchen. The candles, stuck into a motley assortment of holders, sat on the counter, along with a pack of matches. Georgia carried three into the living room, setting one on the table next to Miz Callie and the others on the mantel.

As she did so, lightning cracked in a spectacular display over the water, lighting up the beach for a split second. Then the power went off.

"That was fast." Georgia groped her way back to her grandmother, fumbled with the matches and lit the candle. She made quick work of lighting the other two, welcoming their soft yellow glow.

"Thank you, sugar." Miz Callie patted the overstuffed hassock next to her, and Georgia sat down. "There now, all safe and cozy."

A roll of thunder sounded, so loud it seemed to rattle the dishes in the cupboard. Georgia moved a little closer to her grandmother. "This is just like old times. How many summer thunderstorms have we waited out in here?"

Her grandmother chuckled softly. "Remember when Amanda hid under the bed?"

"I sure do. But it's probably not safe to remind her of that anymore." The polished, efficient Amanda she'd lunched with bore little resemblance to the terrified child who'd refused to come out from under the bed in a storm.

"This house stood through Hugo. I don't reckon anything short of that will bother it."

Sorrow touched her grandmother's face for a moment, and Georgia knew she was thinking about her own family home. Before Hurricane Hugo, it had been on the lot beyond where Matt's rental house stood.

"I'm sorry. You lost so much in Hugo."

"Plenty of people did." Miz Callie patted her hand. "I just hope Lindsay's not frightened. Maybe I should have warned Matt to have some candles ready."

"I'm sure he's capable of handling the situation." The mention of his name brought back those moments on the beach. She wrapped her fingers around her wrist. She could feel his grasp, see the play of emotion in his eyes.

Miz Callie leaned back in the rocker, her gaze on Georgia's face. "I s'pose it's too soon, but I can't help but wonder…"

"Nothing new to report yet. Matt is searching the military records as a starting point." She needed to do her part—to get Miz Callie talking in hopes that more would emerge. "If there's anything else you can remember about that time, it might help."

"I've been thinking about that." She took something from the bookcase behind her. "I had a look around today, and I found this."

Georgia took the book she held out—an old leather album, its cover watermarked. She opened it carefully. The brittle pages cracked at a touch, and some of the photos had washed out so much that they were indecipherable, especially by candlelight.

"They're in a bad way, I'm afraid." Miz Callie touched a faded picture. "That's my mamma and my little sister, your Great-aunt Lizbet. Mamma and Daddy bought me that little Brownie camera for my birthday, and I was so proud of it. Never stopped taking pictures that whole summer."

"The summer Ned left?" A little shiver of excitement went through her.

Her grandmother looked surprised. "That's right, it must have been, because that's the year I got the camera, 1942. We had a crab boil on the beach, I remember, but we had to have it before sunset because of the blackout."

"Blackout?"

"Georgia Lee, don't tell me you didn't know there were blackout regulations during the war." Miz Callie shook her head at such ignorance.

Georgia flushed. "I knew. I just didn't think about it affecting your having a fire on the beach, I guess." It seemed incredibly long ago to her, but obviously not to her grandmother.

"Goodness, child, that was crucial, because of the

U-boats. German submarines," she added, as if doubting Georgia would know the term.

"You mean you were actually in danger here?"

Her grandmother's gaze misted. "They sank ships along the coast from here up to Cape Cod, so I've heard. Grown-ups would stop talking about it when we came into the room. But we knew. We talked about what we'd do if the Germans landed. Your granddad was going to fight them off with his slingshot, as I recall."

Miz Callie's words made it all too real. Her skin prickled, and she rubbed her arm. "I can't imagine living through that."

"You mustn't think we were frightened all the time. Land, no. We played on the beach just like we always did—a whole crew of us kids. We just weren't allowed to roam as far as we wanted—there was a gunnery range from Station 28 all the way up to Breech's Inlet, and of course they expanded Fort Moultrie down at the other end."

She tried to picture it. "You were living right in the middle of a military installation, it sounds like. I'm surprised your folks stayed on the island."

"Pride, I guess. My daddy used to say that Hitler wasn't going to chase him out of his house." Miz Callie smiled, as if she could still hear her daddy's voice. "Folks took it personally, you know. I guess that's why the family was so upset with Ned."

"Did you know that at the time?"

Her grandmother turned a page in the album, frowning down at it. "I think maybe us kids knew something was going on, even if we didn't know what it was. We were in and out of each other's houses, and we'd hear things. I remember Ned's daddy being in an awful mood, it seemed." She pointed to a faded photo. "There we are—the whole bunch of us."

The photo was a five by seven, so it was a little easier to see than the others. Kids in swimsuits, the front row kneeling in the sand. She picked out Miz Callie and Granddad without any trouble. She put her finger on a tall figure in the second row. "Is that Ned?"

Miz Callie nodded. "Fine-looking boy, wasn't he? And there's my cousin Jessie, and the Whitcomb boys—my, I haven't thought of them in years."

This might be exactly what she needed, and there seemed no way to ask the question except to blurt it out. "Are any of them still around?"

"My sister Lizbet, down in Beaufort, you know that." She touched the young faces with her finger. "I don't know about the Whitcomb boys. They were good friends of your granddad and Ned, but they moved away to Atlanta, I think. Tommy Barton— he was Ned's pal. He got into the army that next winter, died somewhere in the South Pacific."

All those young faces, their lives encapsulated in a few brief sentences. Georgia glanced at her grandmother, another question on her lips. But she stifled it. Miz Callie had tears in her eyes, and the finger that touched the photo was trembling.

Georgia clasped her hand. "Will you let me borrow the album for a few days? Adam has a scanner, and I know he'd be glad to scan the pictures into his photo program on the computer. He can probably restore them, at least a bit. Okay?"

Miz Callie nodded, leaning back in the chair. "You do that, sugar. We'll look at them again. Maybe I'll remember somethin' useful."

"You've already helped." She rose, bending to kiss her grandmother's cheek. "We'll work it out. I promise."

Chapter Eight

Matt hesitated on the dock at the Isle of Palms Marina, watching as Georgia stepped lightly onto the deck of a small boat. When he didn't immediately follow her, she looked at him, eyebrows lifting.

"Is something wrong?"

"You're sure you know how to drive this thing?" He grabbed a convenient piling, using it to steady himself as he negotiated the transfer to the boat. Falling into the water wouldn't do a thing for his confidence level.

"Positive." Her face relaxed in a grin. "Trust me, Adam wouldn't let me take his boat if he weren't sure I knew how to handle it. He taught me himself, and he was a tough taskmaster. He had me in tears more than once, but I learned."

"Adam is the brother that's in the Coast Guard,

isn't he?" He slid onto the seat, hoping he could get through this day without making a fool of himself.

"They both are." She bent over a locker and came up with two life vests, tossing him one. "But sometimes I think Adam has saltwater in his veins. It's not enough for him that his work is on the water—his play has to be, too."

She moved to the seat behind the controls, tugging her ball cap down over her forehead. With white shorts showing off her tanned legs and that well-worn Cooper River Run T-shirt, she didn't look much like the Atlanta businesswoman he'd originally thought her to be.

"Do you want me to do anything?" Assuming there was anything here he could do.

"Just sit still." Moving with easy grace, she cast off the lines. In a moment the boat pulled away from the dock.

Georgia concentrated on steering them through the maze of boats in the marina, and he concentrated on her, impressed by her competence. He just liked watching competence. This wasn't about Georgia.

Lying to yourself doesn't help, he thought. When Miz Callie had suggested he have a look at the island property, he'd quickly agreed. Then he'd discovered that her plans included having Georgia take him there by boat.

If he could have found a way out, he'd have taken it. Georgia Bodine was too disturbing to his peace of mind. Every time he thought he had a grip on who she was and how to deal with her, she showed him another aspect of herself.

And he was beginning to like all aspects of Georgia Lee Bodine.

This trip was business, he reminded himself. All he had to do was keep it on that plane, and he'd be fine.

Georgia didn't speak again until they were clear of the marina and out into the channel. Then she gave him a questioning glance. "You don't seem very comfortable on the water. I always thought there was a lot of boating in the Boston area."

Not in his neighborhood, where an open fire hydrant provided the most water he'd seen. "I never got into it, unless you count the swan boats on the Common."

"I've seen pictures of them. They look like fun."

"Not like this." He lifted his face to the breeze. "I didn't realize we had to go by boat to see your grandmother's property."

"Consider it a bonus," Georgia suggested. She pointed off to the side ahead of them. "Look. Bottlenose dolphins."

He leaned forward, watching as two sleek gray dolphins arced through the water, wearing their perpetual smiles as if they were enjoying themselves.

"It looks as if they're keeping pace with us."

"They probably are." Georgia's face glowed with pleasure. "They're very social."

Her expression moved him. She was in her element here. "You love this."

"Who wouldn't?" She gave a sigh of pure pleasure. "I never miss a chance to get out on the water."

"Then why did you leave?"

She shrugged, turning so that the bill of her cap hid her face from him. "I went where the job was, that's all."

He had a feeling that wasn't all. But he didn't want to know, remember? He didn't need to get any closer to Georgia than he already was.

The boat slowed slightly, and she pointed again, as if showing him the sights would keep him off the subject of her personal life. "That's an osprey's nest on that post. They don't seem bothered by all the boat traffic."

"Wish I'd brought a camera. Your grandmother has Lindsay fascinated with the coastal wildlife. She's always asking questions I can't answer."

"I could take her out sometime. Or you could take her on an organized tour to Capers Island. Kids love that."

"Capers Island?" Once again, he was sounding ignorant of his new surroundings.

"It's a state heritage preserve, one of the few untouched barrier islands. What my grandmother has planned for her property is going to be similar, except that she owns just part of an island." She swung the boat in a wide semicircle. "Which we're coming up on now."

The island emerged from the water as they drew closer—a stretch of sandy beach littered with driftwood, dunes covered by wavy sea grass, then the trees: live oaks, palmettos and pines.

Georgia headed straight for it, with no dock in sight. He found he was gripping the side rail.

"Where do we dock?"

"We don't." She eased back on the throttle, so that they rocked gently toward the beach. "Actually there is a dock up one of the tidal creeks, but we usually just pull right in to the beach."

Sure enough, in a moment or two they were on the beach, shoes in hand. Georgia groped in her backpack and pulled out a bottle of insect repellent. "Better douse yourself pretty well. The bugs can be fierce out here."

Following orders, he rubbed the repellent on every inch of exposed skin and pulled his hat down on his forehead. She did the same, then put the bottle away and slung the backpack on her shoulder.

"Okay, let's go. Miz Callie says I should show you everything, so we'd best do as she says."

He fell into step beside her. "Sand, water, dunes... What else do I have to remember?"

Georgia waded into the water, bent, and came up with something in her hand. "Tell her you felt a starfish wiggle." She put the creature onto his hand, where it tickled gently.

He couldn't help but grin.

"I remember the first time Miz Callie put one on my hand." Her smile was soft. "I wasn't much more than three. First I was scared. Then I wanted to keep it for a pet. She explained that we can enjoy all the wonderful creatures God created, but that He has put them where they should be."

The words were simple, but they touched something deep inside him. "She still follows that," he murmured, thinking of the turtles.

Georgia nodded. Taking the starfish, she stooped to put it gently back where it belonged. "Miz Callie would think this a wasted trip if all you came back with was facts about the case."

"Well, the case is important. So is my job."

He'd told himself that concentrating on work would keep him from making a foolish mistake where Georgia was concerned, but with every second, making a foolish mistake seemed more likely.

"I understand." She tilted her head back as she said the words, looking up at him.

His heart lurched, and he took an instinctive step back. He hadn't felt like that since Jennifer. He didn't want to—didn't expect to, ever feel that way again.

"Do you—does your family often come here?"

If Georgia was disappointed in his reaction, she didn't show it. She washed her hand off in the surf.

"We did all the time when we were kids. We'd

come out for the day, look for turtle nests, fish and kayak. The boys would bring along lines and chicken necks to catch crabs, and we'd end with a crab boil on the beach. I always thought—" She stopped, shook her head. "I guess I thought that would go on forever. But we all grew up, got too busy with lives and careers."

He couldn't imagine a childhood that would provide memories like that. "I ought to be doing things like that with Lindsay."

"You can."

"She's shut away from me." The words came out before he could censor them. "I didn't get close enough to her before Jennifer died, and now I can't break through."

He shouldn't have said it. He didn't—couldn't—open his heart to anyone.

"You can't give up." Georgia leaned toward him, her voice passionate. "She's still adjusting to life without her mother. She'll grow to depend on you more and more. You have to believe that."

Georgia's brown eyes had filled with such caring that he was drowning in it, sinking into warmth and comfort that he hadn't known in longer than he could remember. The ice that had encapsulated his heart for so long seemed to shiver and splinter.

She reached out, and her hand touched his arm. Her touch reverberated through him, echoing in his body.

He couldn't look away from her. The water washed

over their feet, warm and caressing, and the sun beat down on them, bringing out the faint freckles that dusted her cheeks.

He touched her shoulder, feeling her skin smooth and warm under his hand, and drew her closer. His heart was pounding in his ears so loudly that surely she must be able to hear it.

He shouldn't. But he was going to. His lips found hers.

For a moment she didn't respond. Then she leaned into the kiss, her hands on his arms, her face tilted to his. She tasted like salt and sunshine and the mysterious ocean, and he didn't want to let her go.

Georgia couldn't be sure who drew back first. Was it her, or was it Matt? Given the fact that she still leaned toward him, her heart thudding, she suspected she hadn't done it.

She forced herself to look into his face, half-afraid of what she might read there. He was gazing down at her, his hands still warm on her arms, an expression that mingled surprise and concern in his eyes. He must be as startled by what had happened between them as she was.

The moment stretched out, the silence growing, weighted with meaning. One of them should speak, but she felt intuitively that whatever was said now could affect their relationship for a long time to come.

"I…" She stopped, clearing her suddenly parched throat. "I didn't expect that."

Didn't she? Certainly she had been aware of the strong current between them, like the tide running high.

Had she ever felt anything like that with James? Even the thought seemed disloyal to James. She'd loved him, hadn't she? But she couldn't ignore this.

Matt raised one hand to brush a wisp of hair back from her face, his touch as gentle as the breeze. His fingers lingered for a moment against her skin.

Then his hand dropped to his side, and he took a step back, his expression suddenly guarded.

"I didn't, either." He shook his head. "I shouldn't have done that." His smile flickered faintly. "Not that I didn't enjoy it. But Lindsay—"

"It's too soon," she said quickly. "For me, too."

She tried to picture James's face, but the image was fading. He'd never been part of her life here— that was why. He represented Atlanta and the pressure cooker that had been their business routine. He had no place in island life, attuned to the rhythm of the sea.

"Right." He took a breath, running his hand through his sun-streaked hair as if trying to clear his mind. "We're agreed, then."

She nodded, trying to ignore a spasm of hurt that he could dismiss it so readily. "We should get on with the tour."

He fell into step with her as she started down the beach. Despite what he'd said, he reached for her hand, surprising her. His fingers entwined with hers so that they were palm to palm, and every fiber of her body seemed to react to the strength of his hand.

She forced herself to concentrate. "This could be similar to Capers Island, if that's Miz Callie's idea."

"She's told me she wants it preserved in as natural a state as possible." He frowned a little. "But she wants some sort of marker as a dedication to your great-uncle."

Georgia tried not to wince. "Just ahead you can see the highest part of the island. That seems the logical site for something like that."

Matt looked where she pointed, at the gentle rise of land beyond the dunes, where the trees began. Then his gaze shifted, and he stared at the beach ahead with an awed expression. "What on earth is that?"

The disbelief in his voice made her smile. She'd forgotten how strange the sight was the first time someone came upon it.

"The boneyard—that's what the locals call it."

"I can see why." Matt approached the closest downed tree, its massive trunk bleached white and rubbed as smooth as a bone by the water and the sun. "It looks like a dinosaur graveyard."

"It does, doesn't it?" Pleased at the comparison, she grasped a branch and pulled herself up to sit on it. "I remember having dreams—nightmares, really—after the first time I came here. Cole told me some wild story about how it really was a graveyard, and naturally I believed him."

Matt seemed to be counting the numbers of downed trees that covered the stretch of beach. "But what caused this? Why did all these trees end up here? A storm?"

She shrugged. "Not necessarily. The coast is constantly changing—washing away in one place, building up in another. You just notice it more on the outermost barrier islands." She ran her hand along smooth, sun-warmed wood. "Something about the way the tide flows makes downed trees wash up here. Eerie, isn't it?"

"I'll say." He hoisted himself up next to her. "I'm beginning to see why this piece of land is such a treasure to Miz Callie."

"It's been in her family for quite a few generations." She hesitated. "You have to understand, nobody has designs on it. They'd all be happy to see her donate it to the state or turn it into a nature preserve."

"The name is the problem."

"Yes. I wish I could see a happy ending with all of this, but I can't. Just a major family row." She shivered a little, in spite of the heat of the sun.

His hand, planted on the trunk, brushed hers lightly. "That really upsets you." It was a statement, not a question.

She tried to smile. "I hate battles. I've never been good at confronting people. The thought makes me want to hide under the bed."

He was silent for a moment.

"Is that what went wrong with your engagement?" he finally asked.

She couldn't possibly take offense at the question, not when his voice was filled with such caring.

"Maybe that was part of it." Would it have made a difference if she had been angry instead of hurt, if she'd lashed out at James instead of running away?

She hesitated, Matt's question echoing in her heart. She'd thought she didn't want to talk about it, but the urge to tell him was strong.

"If I'm out of line…"

She shook her head. "It's all right." She tried to smile. "I'm afraid it's a pretty clichéd story, though."

"Another woman?"

"James wasn't tempted by other women. What drove him was being successful." Even as she said it, she knew how true that was. Why hadn't she seen it sooner—before she was engaged, for instance?

"Plenty of people want to be successful." Matt

said the words mildly enough, but she could hear an edge under them, as if she'd criticized him.

She stared down at her feet, bare and sandy, dangling from the branch. "That's true. I just don't think that excuses claiming someone else's work as your own."

His fingers brushed the back of her hand. "Yours?"

She nodded, not wanting to look at him. "Maybe it wasn't as big a deal as I thought. Maybe I made too much of it. But when I realized what he'd done—well, I just couldn't look at him the same way again. And then, when something went wrong with his project, he laid the blame on me. Which accounts for my current jobless state."

"I didn't realize. What did he say when you confronted him?"

She swallowed. "I didn't. I couldn't." She shot a sideways glance at him. "I told you I wasn't any good at confrontation."

The corner of his mouth twitched. "You didn't seem to have any trouble confronting me."

Georgia laughed. "That was different. I thought you were trying to cheat my grandmother."

"And you'd do anything for her."

"Of course." She might doubt herself in other ways, but she never doubted her commitment to Miz Callie.

His arm came around her shoulders, holding her close, warm and strong. Comforting.

The words came out on an impulse. "You aren't the person I thought you were."

His smile reached his eyes, lighting them. "Neither are you, Georgia Lee. Neither are you."

Chapter Nine

She was like one of the ghost crabs, Georgia decided several days later. Running to duck into a hole in the sand at the slightest sign of any disturbance in her world.

She stood at the sliding glass door, looking out at waves foaming gently on the shore. Miz Callie sat in her beach chair, her battered straw hat perched on her head. As a concession to the growing heat, her striped beach umbrella was tilted at an angle to block the sun. Lindsay, a few yards away, was intent on her sand castle.

Georgia shoved the door open and stepped outside. Her own thoughts weren't particularly good company. She'd join them and talk about something—anything—else.

She trotted down the steps, grabbed a beach chair from underneath the deck and walked down to them.

Miz Callie looked up with a welcoming smile. "Glad you decided to come out."

Georgia sank into the chair, tilting her face toward the breeze. "I feel as if I ought to be doing something more useful than sitting here."

"Nonsense. You need a little rest." Miz Callie shot her a shrewd glance. "Any chance you're ready now to tell me what happened when you and Matt went to the island?"

"I…I don't know what you mean." She'd always thought her grandmother could read her thoughts, and this just proved it. "I told you what we did."

"Sugar, taking a tour of the property isn't enough to make you as distracted as you've been ever since you got back. If you don't want to tell me, you can always say I should mind my own business."

"I would never say that." And she didn't want to. She valued her grandmother's solid wisdom too much for that. "I told Matt about what happened with James."

"I thought you might."

"Well, I didn't. I didn't expect to tell him. I hardly know him."

But she had, and his reaction had surprised her. She could still feel the warm, comforting weight of his arm around her shoulders.

"At a guess, I'd say he understood."

"Yes." He'd understood—or at least he hadn't

blamed her for feeling she couldn't go on with James once she realized his true character.

"He's a good man," Miz Callie said. "In spite of being from up north. A little too private, but he has integrity."

The way Miz Callie said it left no doubt that she valued that quality highly.

Georgia stared at a shrimp boat making its way slowly parallel to the shore, its nets down. "I thought maybe he'd feel I should have been glad to further James's career. That's what Mamma said. It's James's career that's important. He was trying to get ahead for my sake. Wasn't I willing to sacrifice for him?"

The words came out in a rush, and she hadn't realized until this moment how much they'd rankled, like a splinter she couldn't get out.

"Maybe she's right. Maybe I didn't love him enough to sacrifice for him."

"Don't be foolish, child." Miz Callie's voice was as tart as it ever got. "If he'd come to you, asked you to help him, of course you'd have done it, wouldn't you?"

She nodded. Of course she would. "That wasn't James's way. He didn't ask. He took."

"Not a good quality in a husband, I'd say. And if your mamma had thought it through, she'd say the same. Goodness, she wouldn't want someone like that in the family."

Wouldn't she? Georgia wasn't so sure of that, but she felt stronger knowing that Miz Callie understood.

Lindsay came running up to them and flopped down on a towel at Miz Callie's feet. "Hot." She pushed damp hair back from her forehead.

"You need to spend a little time in the shade, sugar." Miz Callie handed her a water bottle. "Goodness, what was I thinkin', letting you stay out in the heat this long?"

Lindsay leaned against her knee. "Tell me a story, please? About when you were a little girl on the island."

Georgia's attention sharpened. That was what she wanted to hear, too, but they had different reasons.

Miz Callie smiled, her eyes seeming to focus on the past. "When I was a little girl, the island was so different, you couldn't imagine." The smile faded a little. "That was a long time ago, back in the 1940s. We were at war then." She touched Lindsay's hair lightly. "I pray you never have to experience that."

"I know about that. I have a doll that my Grammy gave me, with a book about living then."

"It was hard all over. Here, the military took over a lot of the island. Why, there were folks in uniform everywhere you looked, and big guns along the shore in places."

Lindsay's eyes grew wide. "What were the guns for?"

"Folks said the enemy might bring their submarines in real close." Miz Callie caught herself, probably thinking that might not be a suitable story for a child. "Anyway, it was exciting for us kids. We played just like we always had, except for our parents being more particular about us getting in early."

"I don't like to go in while it's still light out," Lindsay observed. "Except Daddy lets me watch television."

"We didn't have television then, you know. We had the radio, and sometimes we'd listen to that." She shook her head. "Funny. I s'pose the parents listened to the news, but all I remember hearing is the music. 'Tangerine,' played by the Jimmy Dorsey band. That was one we listened to over and over."

Miz Callie's memory of those days seemed to be getting clearer and clearer.

"Did you go swimming in the ocean?" Lindsay prompted, apparently not interested in long-ago radio programs.

"We went swimming, sure thing. And crabbing. We loved to go crabbing. One of the older boys would take us." A faint shadow crossed her face, and Georgia knew she was thinking of Ned. "We'd bring back a mess of crabs and then have a crab boil, right here on the beach."

"That sounds so fun." Lindsay's tone was wistful. "I wish I could do that."

"Maybe you will." Miz Callie leaned back in the chair, her eyes closing.

For an instant she looked her age, and Georgia's heart hurt. Did Miz Callie want to share her memories because she feared one day soon she wouldn't be able to?

"Maybe you ought to go in and take a rest." Georgia made the suggestion tentatively, knowing how little Miz Callie liked being told what to do. "It is awful hot today."

Her grandmother planted her hands on the arms of her chair. "I haven't checked the nest yet. I have to make sure those visitors haven't been back, fooling with it again."

"I'll do that." She rose as her grandmother did, touching her arm. "Lindsay and I will do that for you, won't we, Lindsay?"

The child scrambled to her feet. "Sure we will, Miz Callie. We'll take care of it."

Miz Callie split a smile between the two of them. "Well, then, I guess I can't say no. Ya'll come in and have some nice cold lemonade when you get back, y'heah?"

She'd suggest Miz Callie lie down for a while, but that wouldn't be well received. "Yes, ma'am. And I'll bring the chairs and umbrella when I come, so just leave them."

To her surprise, that didn't lead to an argument. Her grandmother nodded and walked slowly toward the house.

Lindsay watched her as intently as Georgia. "Is Miz Callie sick?" Anxiety filled her voice.

The poor child—she'd had enough losses.

"I'm sure she'll be fine once she gets inside where it's cool. Ready to check the nest?"

Lindsay slipped her feet into the sandals she'd discarded while building her castle. "I'm ready."

They walked down the beach together. It was easy enough to spare Miz Callie by checking the nest. Not so easy to resolve the bigger burden that weighed on her. So far they'd come up with exactly nothing to explain why Ned had left or what had happened to him afterward.

"A lot of people Miz Callie knows died, didn't they?"

The child's voice was so solemn that for an instant Georgia wondered if she was talking about Ned. But no, they hadn't discussed that in front of her.

"I guess so." Since she didn't know what prompted the question, she'd better be cautious in her answer. "Miz Callie's lived a long time. She'd say that it's natural that some folks she loved would go ahead of her to Heaven."

"But it makes her sad. And mad sometimes, too." Lindsay's face wore an expression of utmost concentration. They were no longer talking about Miz Callie. They were talking about Lindsay and her losses.

"I'm sure it makes her feel sad and angry sometimes," she said carefully. "But she knows they're safe with Jesus, and she knows she'll see them again someday."

"That's what my grammy says about my mommy." Lindsay's lips pressed together, as if to hold something back.

"Does that make you angry?" She ventured a question, knowing she was out of her depth.

"No." Lindsay snapped the word, her face assuming a stoic facade.

Like the one Matthew wore at times. Somehow she didn't think stoicism was working well for either of them.

Dear Lord, show me what to say to this child. She's hurting more than I imagined, and I haven't the faintest idea how to help her.

And she didn't have the right to help her, either— it felt like she was interfering. But did that matter, if Lindsay turned to her?

"Lindsay…"

Before she could find any words, Lindsay darted across the sand. "There's the nest," she cried.

Georgia followed, half relieved, half sorry that Lindsay wasn't going to open up to her after all.

"Everything looks okay." Georgia tightened the

tape on one of the sticks. "I don't think anybody has bothered it."

"Have to make sure." Lindsay made a circle around the nest, touching each stick with her fingers.

Georgia's heart clenched. It reminded her of that first day, when she'd watched the child lining up the seashells just so.

Her circuit done, Lindsay sat down where Miz Callie always sat when she visited the nest. With another silent prayer for guidance, Georgia sat down next to her.

Lindsay stared at the nest. "We have to take care of the baby turtles." Her face was solemn. "They don't have anyone else."

Please, Lord, her heart murmured. "The mamma turtle put the eggs in a safe place. Unless someone comes along and bothers it—"

"She went away!" The words burst out of Lindsay. "Their mother just went away and left them."

Her heart seemed to be lodged in her throat. "That's in the nature of sea turtles," she said slowly, carefully. "The mamma turtles travel a very long way to lay their eggs on the same beach every year. That's what their instinct tells them to do."

She dared a look at Lindsay, praying she was taking the right tack with her. The child sat with her knees pulled up, arms wrapped around them. Her head was bent, her hair falling forward to expose the nape of her neck.

The sight of that pale, fragile column did funny things to Georgia. The urge to protect stormed through her, taking her breath away with its strength.

She's not my responsibility. Instinct, compelling as the instinct that drove the turtles, countered that feeble claim. Lindsay had come to her—why, she didn't know. She had to find a way to help her.

"People aren't turtles." Lindsay whispered the words. "They're not s'posed to leave their children."

She touched the curve of the child's back. "No, people aren't meant to be like that. Mammas want to protect and help their children grow." She took a deep breath. "But sometimes they can't, no matter how much they might want to."

"I didn't want my mom to die." There was still that trace of anger in the words.

"Of course you didn't, sugar." The touch turned into a caress. To her surprise, Lindsay didn't pull away. "You know, it's natural to feel angry with your mamma for dying, even though you know it wasn't her fault."

Silence for a moment. "That's what Dr. Annie said."

"Dr. Annie sounds like a wise woman." Obviously Matt had tried to get professional help for his daughter.

"I guess." Her mouth clamped shut on the words. The shield came down over her expression again. It was as if the tide were carrying her away, and Georgia couldn't reach her now, no matter how she tried.

"Lindsay…"

This time the child did pull away from her touch, but she had to keep trying, even if it did no good.

"Lindsay, you should talk to your daddy about how you're feeling. He'd understand, really he would."

She shook her head, her face stoic. "I can't. He'd get upset. I can't." She jumped to her feet. "I have to go."

"Wait." But it was too late. Lindsay was already running down the beach.

Running to find a hole to hide in. She understood the feeling. It was what she did, all too often. She couldn't, not now. If she were going to help Lindsay, to say nothing of Miz Callie, she'd have to stop hiding and start speaking her mind.

Georgia hadn't imagined, when she'd mentioned going to see Miz Callie's sister in Beaufort, that Matt would have the slightest interest in joining her. She'd been wrong.

At the moment he was frowning as he negotiated the heavy traffic along the strip development on the other side of the Ashley River.

"You really didn't have to come today. I could have talked to my great-aunt on my own."

He shot her a glance, his eyes unreadable behind his sunglasses. "Didn't want me butting in on it?"

"It's not that." He smiled, and she realized he'd been teasing her. She was unaccountably flustered today.

Well, maybe not unaccountably.

She ought to be honest with herself, at least. She'd been aware of Matt's magnetism since the moment they met, when she'd still considered him the enemy. Then, that day they'd played with Lindsay in the surf, she'd felt the pull of attraction between them, strong as the ebb tide.

She'd been able to handle that. But once they'd kissed…

She could still handle it, she assured herself hurriedly. Neither of them was ready for anything serious now, and both of them realized it. That should be protection enough.

"It wasn't a problem to come with you. Lindsay is happy with the sitter your grandmother recommended. I just feel I haven't done enough for Miz Callie," Matt said. "Not nearly enough."

There was an undercurrent in his voice that she didn't entirely understand.

"You've set the wheels in motion for turning the land into a preserve, just as she wants."

He shrugged, hands moving a little restlessly on

the steering wheel. "That, sure. Any lawyer could do that for her. What she really wants is to find out what happened to Ned. That's where I've let her down."

His concern touched her. He really did care about her grandmother as more than just a client.

"I can't say I've done any better. It's felt fairly hopeless from the beginning."

He nodded. They'd passed the last of the development now, and the road stretched ahead, bordered only by tall pines and live oaks with their swags of Spanish moss.

"You know..." He hesitated. "We haven't really talked about how to handle it if Miz Callie is wrong. If everyone else believes that Ned was a coward who ran away rather than fight..." He shrugged. "There has to be some basis for that belief."

"Miz Callie believes in Ned."

"And you?"

"Let's say I'm trying to have faith that she's right."

He gave her a half smile that did funny things to her heart. "I've heard it said that faith is believing when common sense tells you not to."

"'The substance of things hoped for,'" she quoted softly. "I guess I'm praying that, as well."

The silence stretched between them for a moment. It would have been natural for him to reply in kind, but he hadn't. Because he didn't believe?

Surely it wasn't that. He sent Lindsay to Bible school, and Miz Callie said he'd come to church with her several times.

"Those war years seem far away to me," he said in what Georgia thought was a deliberate attempt to change the subject. "I've done some reading since Miz Callie got me involved. None of my school history courses ever got as far as World War II."

"I know what you mean." If he needed to shy away from the subject of faith, she had to respect that. "We'd make it to the Roaring Twenties if we were lucky, and then school would be out and the next year we'd start with Columbus again. Most of my ideas about the war come from old movies."

He nodded, frowning at a motorcyclist who had just swung widely around them. For an instant she saw him as one of those gallant heroes off to fight. A hint of something tough and ready for battle under Matt's civilized exterior made him fit the part.

Who was he, really, under that facade he wore so well? She'd had glimpses from time to time, but all they served to do was whet her curiosity.

He'd come through adversity—she could see that in the lines around his eyes and the wary expression he wore so often.

At first she'd thought that was the effect of his wife's death, but she'd begun to believe it ran deeper. She'd never know, unless he let her. The massive control he exerted kept his feelings well hidden.

His daughter was trying to emulate his control, and it wasn't working for her.

Georgia's heart twisted. Poor child. Had anything she'd said to Lindsay helped at all? She doubted it.

Matt was the only one who could help. Someone had to talk to him about it.

Not me. Please, Father. I wouldn't be any good at it.

That selfish prayer got just the answer it deserved. She knew what she had to do. Had known since those moments with Lindsay at the turtle nest.

She fought to quell the nervous tremor that came from deep inside her. If she had to be the one to bring it up, she would, but after they'd talked to her great-aunt, not before. One difficult conversation at a time was plenty.

When the landmarks began to appear, she leaned forward. "Have you been to Beaufort yet?"

"Afraid not. I've been too busy with work to take any side trips."

"You're in for a treat, then. Great-aunt Lizbet claims it's the most beautiful town on the coast, and there are plenty who'd agree with her. Not a Charlestonian, of course."

"Of course," he said with mock seriousness and a hint of a smile. "I've already noticed how humble Charlestonians are about their city."

"It's yours, too, now."

He didn't say anything for a moment, then shrugged. "I guess adoption may take a few generations."

The busy outskirts of Beaufort gave way suddenly to the gracious old town with its antebellum houses and hundred-year-old live oaks.

"We turn left at the next light." Maybe a warning was in order. "Miz Callie and her sister aren't much alike. And Lizbet is a couple of years younger, so I'm not sure we can expect her to remember much. She might not have known the same people."

He negotiated the turn. "At this point, any lead is a good one."

She tried to hang on to that thought as they pulled to the side of the road in front of her great-aunt's house. Graceful old trees arched over the street adding an air of serenity.

Matt walked around the car to join her at the gate. "I feel as if we've stepped back a couple of centuries."

"Me, too. Progress passed Beaufort by, and I think the town is the better for it."

She started to open the gate, but Matt reached around her to do it, his arm brushing hers. A wave of warmth swept over her skin at the simple touch. He smiled down at her.

She took a breath. She'd better put on a little armor—Aunt Lizbet had an unquenchable urge to spot romance in the most unlikely duos. Georgia preceded Matt up the walk, trying not to notice his protective hand on her elbow as she negotiated the uneven flagstone walk.

"Aunt Lizbet better get those stones fixed before one of her cronies takes a tumble on them." Trying to ignore the slightly breathless sound of her voice, she went up the four steps to the wide, gracious porch. She had to be careful, very careful. And not just because of the uneven walk.

Chapter Ten

The door was flung open, and Aunt Lizbet threw her arms around Georgia in an exuberant hug. "Here you are at last, Georgia Lee! Goodness, it's about time you're coming to see me. I'd begun to think I'd have to trek way up to the island if I wanted a glimpse of you."

"You ought to come, even if not to see me. I know Miz Callie would love that."

She looked affectionately at her great-aunt. Callie and her sister had a strong family resemblance, but they couldn't be more different in personality. Callie was most at home in cut-offs, sandals and a floppy beach hat, while Lizbet made seasonal trips to Atlanta to replenish an already extensive wardrobe. And while Callie was walking on the beach looking for her beloved turtles, her sister spent her days in a round of social activities that would exhaust a woman half her age.

"You're looking wonderful, Aunt Lizbet." The compliment was true. She was perfection from the delicate blush on her cheeks to the soles of her Italian leather pumps. "You didn't need to dress up for us."

"Oh, darlin', not that I wouldn't have, but you know, my garden club is coming for a meeting in an hour." She turned toward Matt. "And who's this? Have you replaced that fiancé of yours already?"

Her own cheeks were suddenly pinker than anything Aunt Lizbet's blush could achieve. "This is Matthew Harper. He's taking care of some legal work for Miz Callie. Matt, this is my great-aunt, Elizabeth Dayton."

Aunt Lizbet extended her hand as if she expected it to be kissed. Matt shook hands with a faint twinkle of amusement in his eyes.

"Mrs. Dayton, it's a pleasure. Thank you for inviting us to your home."

"Well, now, the pleasure is all mine, especially when Georgia brings such a handsome young man." She batted her eyelashes in her most extravagant manner, knowing perfectly well she was being outrageous. If Matt hadn't figured out by now that her family tree was filled with eccentrics, he was a lot slower than she'd given him credit for being.

"Behave yourself, Auntie." Georgia put her arm around her great-aunt's waist. "If your garden club is coming in an hour, we don't have time to waste on flirting."

"Flirting is never a waste, darlin'." Aunt Lizbet patted her cheek and swept another glance over Matt. "Next you'll be telling me that I'm too old for him."

"I'm afraid I might be too old for you, Miz Dayton," Matt said smoothly. Georgia was enjoying this gallant Matt—he was full of surprises.

Clearly flattered, her great-aunt led the way into her parlor. "Georgia, sugar, you need to snap this one up right away."

If she got any redder, she might just go up in flames. "I just broke my engagement. I'm not—"

"Oh, poof, what's a little broken engagement? Why, a girl has to have a few discarded sweethearts in her wake, or how's she going to know she's got the right one?"

"You stop playing Scarlett O'Hara for a minute and sit down." She tried her best to frown at her great-aunt, but it was impossible. It would be like frowning at the frilly, unlikely angel on top of the Christmas tree. "We've got to get our business taken care of before your ladies descend upon us."

Matt took the seat her great-aunt indicated, looking slightly appalled at the thought of a whole garden club full of Scarlett O'Haras, and Georgia sat next to her on the rose velvet loveseat. It was hard to concentrate seriously on anything in Aunt Lizbet's parlor, decorated as it was in the very

height of Victorian whimsy by some earlier generation of Daytons, and accented by her great-aunt
with Dresden shepherdesses and lacy pillows.

"Miz Callie has asked Matt to try and find out
what happened to Uncle Ned—my granddad's
brother, that is…"

"I know who your uncle Ned was, child, even
though he's not related to me, exactly." She tipped
her head to one side. "Let's see, he'd be my sister's
brother-in-law, so that would make him—"

"We hoped you might remember him," Matt
interrupted.

Good, Georgia thought. Let her embark on family
connections, and they'd never get anywhere. "We'd
like to find out what happened to him after he left
Sullivan's Island in 1942."

Aunt Lizbet turned to him with a flattering smile.
"Oh, goodness, so long ago. You might not realize
it, but I'm quite a bit younger than Callie. Why, I
was hardly more than a baby at the time."

Georgia bit her lip to keep herself from pointing
out that, according to the family tree, there were
only eighteen months between them.

"Of course I understand that," Matt said, his
tone soothing. "But sometimes very young children
do remember the oddest things. We're especially
interested in anything that happened that summer
involving Ned."

Her aunt's gaze strayed to the drop-leaf table, already arrayed with a silver bowl of roses and her heavy silver tea service. "I just don't believe I can help."

"That's all right," Georgia said briskly. "I told Matt that you wouldn't have nearly the memory that Miz Callie does, but he insisted we come and see you anyway."

If Matt was surprised, he managed to hide it.

"Callie, indeed!" Aunt Lizbet's indignation peaked. "I remember things twice as well as she does. Anybody who knows us will tell you that I always had the better memory. I won the county spelling bee three years in a row."

"That's a wonderful accomplishment." Matt leaned forward, capturing one of Aunt Lizbet's hands in his own. "I can see we should have come to you right off. Won't you tell us about Ned?"

"Well…" For a moment, she seemed to be at a loss, but then her eyes brightened. "I can tell you something nobody else knows, not even Callie. It was a secret, and I kept it all these years."

Georgia's pulse quickened. A secret? Were they really going to learn something helpful? She opened her mouth and closed it again at a commanding glance from Matt.

Well, all right, if he thought he could get more out of her great-aunt than she could, let him try. Although come to think of it, Aunt Lizbet was far more likely to respond to a handsome man any day of the week.

"It was a rainy evenin', I remember." Aunt Lizbet's hand rested in Matt's. "The others were all inside, listening to the radio, but I went out on the beach."

"By yourself?" Matt prompted.

She nodded. "Mamma wouldn't have let me if I'd asked, so I didn't ask. It wasn't curfew yet, just dark because of the rain. I'd left my pail full of shells where we'd been playing, and I wanted to get it before the tide came in."

There was something soothing and timeless about that, something in common between those children who'd played on the beach in the midst of a war and the ones who played on it today.

"I got the bucket and then stopped there on the dunes for a minute, just looking at the water. Then I saw her." She stopped, as if the image was one she didn't want to see.

"Who was it?" Matt asked softly.

She shook her head. "I don't know. One of the summer people. She'd waded way out in the water with her clothes on. Imagine. She even had a hat on her head, and there she was. All of a sudden a wave knocked her down." Her face puckered in imitation of long-ago distress. "Before I could think what to do, Ned Bodine came running past me. Straight into the water, with his clothes on, too, and swimming out toward her." She smiled, seeming to recall herself to the present. "Funny how that picture is still so fresh in my mind. Ned was always the best swimmer of all the kids."

"He pulled her out?"

"Land, yes. It didn't take him any time at all. Then he brought her up the path, and he saw me and stopped. He patted my cheek, and he said I should go home. And not to tell anyone, because the lady would be embarrassed. It was our secret."

"And you kept it."

She fluttered a little. "Well, truth to tell, I probably forgot about it pretty quick, but there it was, stored in my mind, ready to fall out the minute you asked."

"I'm glad you remembered."

"That's fine, darlin'. I don't suppose it helps you know what happened to Ned, but it's good you know that story." She rose with one of her sudden movements. "Look at the time. I'll get y'all some sweet tea, and then I'm going to have to shoo you out before my ladies get here."

"You don't have to—" Matt began, but she was already gone. He turned to Georgia. "What did you think of that?"

"I think she was telling the exact truth, the way a child would remember something," she said, feeling a little deflated. "But I'm afraid it doesn't get us anywhere."

"I don't agree."

Matt leaned toward her, much as he had leaned toward Aunt Lizbet, and took her hand in his. She hoped her great-aunt hadn't had the breathless reaction that she was having.

"What do you think we found out?" She kept her voice even with an effort.

"We learned something valuable about Ned Bodine," he said. "Whatever he did, and whatever else he was, he certainly wasn't a coward."

"You were right about the restaurant." Matt scrawled his signature on the credit-card receipt and glanced across the table at Georgia, enjoying the sight of her more than he wanted to. "The shrimp burger was amazing."

"I'm glad you liked it. Sorry it was so crowded."

The crowd had kept him from pursuing the topic on both their minds, but maybe that was just as well.

When he'd suggested lunch before they headed back to Charleston, Georgia had directed him to Bay Street, lined with shops, restaurants and elegant old buildings. He'd followed her down a walkway between two buildings and into one of the smallest restaurants he'd ever seen. It offered windows looking out onto the water and food that was well worth the crush.

He touched Georgia's elbow as she rose and nodded toward the back door that opened onto the waterfront park. "Let's stretch our legs before we get back in the car."

For a moment he thought she'd refuse. Then she nodded.

Warm, moist air settled on them the instant they stepped outside, mitigated a little by the breeze off the water. He stole a glance at Georgia's face as they started down the walk toward the low wall that bordered the sound.

She'd seemed tense underneath the surface conversation over lunch. He couldn't think of anything to account for that. The story from her great-aunt, and the conclusion he'd drawn from it, surely hadn't upset her.

They reached the path that ran along the water and turned wordlessly to walk along it. Ahead of them, a father with two young children was attempting to get a kite in the air. Several women, perhaps workers from the shops along the street, sat with sack lunches on park benches, talking, and a pair of intent joggers passed them, earphones blocking out the world.

Did Georgia realize how quiet she was being? Had she been upset by her great-aunt's obvious matchmaking? It was so good-humored, so much a part of the Southern-belle persona she'd put on, that no one could take it seriously.

From the street above them, he could hear the voice of a tour guide perched on the high seat of a horse-drawn carriage. She must have said something amusing, because her carriage of tourists laughed.

He glanced again at Georgia's intent face. They understood each other, didn't they? Understood the attraction they both felt, but recognized that it couldn't go any deeper for either of them?

Still, that didn't mean he couldn't enjoy being with her, watching the way her hair curled rebelliously against her neck, listening to the soft cadences of her voice.

Except that at the moment, she wasn't talking.

"I can understand why your great-aunt loves this place. It really is beautiful," he ventured.

Roused from her abstraction, she smiled. "If she hadn't been so busy playing the Southern belle today, she'd have given you the history of Beaufort in one intensive lecture. Including how many films have been shot here."

"Really?" He wouldn't have pictured the sleepy place as a southern Hollywood.

"Oh, yes." Her smile widened. "Cole and I ditched school one day when they were making a movie, and he drove us down here. We were sure we were going to have a personal encounter with a star."

"Did you?"

"The closest we came was a glimpse of a motor home that might have belonged to the film company.

And a three-week grounding for Cole when we got home."

"Not you?" He liked the affection on her face when she talked about her brothers.

"I only got two, because Cole was older. He was supposed to be more responsible." She paused, watching a sparkling white sailboat move soundlessly past them.

"Cole—that's the brother next to you in age, isn't it?"

She nodded. "He's a jet pilot." Something, some faint shadow, crossed her eyes.

"Dangerous work," he guessed.

"Not as bad as when he was a rescue swimmer, dropping from the chopper into the water. Mamma spent so much time worrying about him that she said she was going to need a face-lift by the time he decided to make the change."

"I take it Cole's a bit of a daredevil."

"Always trying to keep up with Adam."

"And you tried to keep up with both of them, I suppose." A bench swing was mounted facing the water, and he touched her arm to lead her to it, adding the feel of her skin to the list of things he enjoyed about being with her.

She leaned back, tilting her face to the sun. "If my mamma didn't want a tomboy, she shouldn't have had the two boys first." As if she realized she'd betrayed something, she pointed out across the water. "That's Lady's Island. Beyond it is St. Helena's. You ought to drive out there one day. At the very end is Hunting Island State Park. You can stand at the lighthouse and look out at the ocean where streets and houses used to be."

"Another moving barrier island?"

She nodded. "I'm probably telling you things you already know, since you grew up in Boston."

"Not much maritime lore in my part of the city," he said shortly.

"No?" Her eyes widened a little.

He was about to turn the subject away, as he always did. He'd had plenty of practice in avoiding the subject of his childhood.

But somehow, despite his best efforts, he and Georgia had become close. And he couldn't put her off with something that wasn't a lie but wasn't quite the truth, either.

"I don't know what you're imagining," he said slowly. "But just because I went to law school with Rod doesn't mean I grew up in a home like his."

She half turned toward him, her arm brushing his. "I don't know that I was imagining anything. You've learned a good bit about my people since we met, but I don't know anything about yours."

"I don't have people, not in the sense you mean."

Her eyes grew troubled. "But you had parents..."

"My father disappeared before I was born."

Better to get it out bluntly if he was going to tell her. "My mother was an alcoholic who gave up trying to get her life together before I was out of diapers."

"I'm sorry." Her face held compassion, not the shock he was expecting. "How hard that must have been for you."

He shrugged. "If you haven't experienced anything else, you don't know what you're missing."

She rested her hand on his arm, and her empathy flowed through the contact. "You must have known, or you wouldn't have had the drive to become what you are."

"Maybe."

He didn't like to look back at who he'd been then—liked it even less since he'd become a parent himself. It was painful to imagine Lindsay living the way he had—always afraid, always yearning for something he couldn't even imagine.

"Someone helped you." She said it as if she knew. "Someone gave you a goal to strive for."

He nodded. "Several someones, I guess. The pastor at a shelter we stayed in. A teacher who cared. A businessman who thought he should pay back what he'd received by helping someone else."

"God sent them into your life." Her voice was so soft, so gentle, that it flowed over him in a wave of comfort.

"I guess. I mean, yes." For just an instant his

mind clouded. He believed that, didn't he? Since Jennifer died, he'd lost sight of what he believed.

"But you became who you are by your own efforts, too. That shows a lot of character."

He shrugged, not eager to prolong the subject. "I was lucky."

It was too hard to believe that he'd inherited any degree of character from either of his parents.

"Attribute it to luck if you want to, but that's not going to stop me from admiring what you've accomplished." Her voice was firm. "I'm glad you told me."

He still remembered how he'd felt when he'd told Jennifer—he'd been so sure she'd back politely away from their relationship. She hadn't, and her love had made him feel as if he could conquer anything that stood in the way of their happiness.

He'd been wrong.

Seeming to recognize that he'd said all he intended to, Georgia leaned back on the swing.

"Maybe this isn't the right time, but there's something I've been wanting to talk to you about."

He tried to clear his mind of the lingering cobwebs of the past. "Now's as good a time as any. What is it? Something about your grandmother?"

She took a breath, and he realized she was trying to compose herself. This was what had caused her abstraction, then.

His hand brushed hers. "Just tell me, whatever it is."

She looked down so that her hair fell forward, brushing her cheek. "The other day Lindsay and I went to check out the turtle nest together."

At the sound of his daughter's name, everything inside him tensed. "What happened?"

"Nothing happened, exactly." She looked up at him, velvet-brown eyes earnest. "Please understand, I wouldn't ordinarily repeat a conversation with a child. But I think—"

"If it has to do with my daughter, I need to hear it." He chopped off the words, willing her to come out with it.

"She expressed a lot of angry feelings about the mother turtles leaving their babies to fend for themselves. It seemed to me she was talking about her mother's death."

"Did she say that?" She was right. He knew she was right, but he didn't want to admit it, because that meant admitting he hadn't solved this for his child.

Pity filled Georgia's face. "She did. I think she understands that her mamma didn't choose what happened to her, but still—"

"What did you say to her?"

Georgia stiffened, pulling away from him a little. "I didn't pry into her feelings, if that's what you're imagining. It just came out."

He didn't have the right to be mad at Georgia because his daughter had gone to her, not to him.

He forced down the anger that threatened to over-power him.

"Sorry. I didn't mean it that way." He shook his head, as if he could clear it. "She saw a counselor before we moved here. I hoped things were getting better."

"I'm sure they are." Her face warmed, and she leaned toward him, eagerness to help evident in every movement. "I said she should talk to you, but she didn't seem to feel she could. Maybe if you were to share your feelings, she'd think—"

"No." He shot off the seat, leaving it swinging. "Just leave it alone, Georgia. You don't understand."

"Of course." She said the words quietly, but he knew they hid a world of pain. "You have to decide what's best for your daughter." She rose, not looking at him.

He wanted to say something that would wipe the hurt from her eyes. But he couldn't.

He couldn't, because what she suggested was impossible. He'd do anything for his daughter's happiness, anything but open up and expose his own pain, because if he did, the ferocity of it might shatter them both forever.

Chapter Eleven

Matt was right—Georgia didn't understand. She watched the countryside roll past as they drove back toward the island. One moment they were closer than they'd ever been, and the next the doors had slammed shut with a resounding crash.

She'd ventured her opinion on Lindsay. Matt considered his daughter's emotional health out of bounds.

A faint annoyance hovered. Did he really think that she and Miz Callie could spend as much time as they did with Lindsay and not grow to care for her? Maybe she didn't have much experience with children, but she did know what it was like to feel desperate for someone to understand her. That was what Lindsay needed right now, and that someone should be her father.

And if he couldn't or wouldn't? She ventured a

glance at Matt. She knew him well enough now to recognize what a stranger wouldn't—that extra tension in his jaw, the shutters drawn over his expression. He was blocking her out, and her heart ached.

She could try to be the friend that Lindsay needed, but she'd have to tread carefully. Matt could probably be ruthless where protecting his child was concerned, even if he was wrong about what she needed.

They made the turn at Gardens Corners, and he cleared his throat slightly. "How do you think your grandmother will react to her sister's story?"

Apparently they were talking again, now that he'd warned her off.

"She'll probably feel as you do—that it proves Ned wasn't a coward."

"And you don't agree?" He shot her a glance, frowning.

"It proves he had courage, but diving into the waves to rescue someone in trouble would be almost second nature to a person who'd spent his life on the water."

"He'd know the dangers better than anyone."

"True." She spread her hands, palms up. "Okay, he was brave. That doesn't cover all the reasons why he might have run away. Maybe he was opposed to the war."

"I'd expect we'd have heard about that from someone. Your grandmother didn't imply anything like that."

"Miz Callie was a child. She might not have known."

Matt drummed his fingers on the steering wheel. "What we really need is someone who was Ned's contemporary."

She nodded. Absorbed in discussing the problem, she was almost able to forget how Matt had shut her out. Almost. Still, she could set it aside to deal with the immediate issue.

If one could call something that happened more than sixty years ago "immediate."

"I took some of Miz Callie's old photographs to Adam. They'd faded so much that they were practically invisible, but he thought he could bring them up with his photo program. If so, it might prompt her memories about who was around that summer."

"Good idea." He passed a slow-moving truck with concentrated care. "Give me names, and I'll find out what happened to them. They can't all have vanished."

Frustration filled his voice. Matt was a man who set goals and met them, and he didn't tolerate failure readily, in himself and probably not in others.

"It's not your fault. You can't find what's not there."

"He certainly seemed determined to vanish. You'd think he'd have cared about the people he left behind."

"I've been thinking about that, too. Miz Callie describes someone who was kind, attentive to the younger kids in a way that a teenager often isn't."

He darted a glance at her, his mouth quirking in a faint smile. "Speaking from personal experience?"

"Well…" She considered. "My brothers were protective of me, I guess. They wouldn't let anybody else pick on me, but that didn't prevent them from doing it. And there were plenty of times when having me around was the last thing they wanted. You know how siblings are."

The moment the words were out, she wanted them back. The childhood Matt had described hadn't included siblings.

"No, I don't," he said, voice dry.

"I'm sorry. I didn't think."

He shrugged. "It doesn't matter. Anyway, let's see what Miz Callie thinks."

Biting her tongue wasn't going to help. "I'll try to get her talking about that, but again, it's the memory of a young child."

He nodded, frowning as the thickening traffic brought him to halt. "Let's hope your brother comes up with something from the photographs, then. That seems to be our best hope at the moment." He glanced across at her, something questioning in his gaze. "Do you want to keep quiet about the story your Aunt Lizbet told us?"

"No, I didn't mean that. Goodness, we'd never

be able to, not when she knows where we went today." She pressed her palms on her knees. "I just hate to see her getting buoyed up about it, and then being even more disappointed if we can't come up with anything."

"You want to protect her." The tender note in his voice seemed to reach right into her heart.

"Of course I do." She hesitated, not sure how much she wanted to say to him. "She's always done that for me. It's time I did my part."

"Your grandmother has probably dealt with disappointment. I think she knows how to handle it."

Miz Callie was strong. Georgia didn't doubt that. "This is the only thing she's ever asked of me." Her throat thickened. "I don't want to let her down. I won't."

"We can't always protect the people we love from pain."

Was he talking about her grandmother? Or about his daughter? She wasn't sure, and he wouldn't tell her.

Miz Callie had reacted just about the way Georgia had feared when they'd told her about Aunt Lizbet's story. In fact, she'd kept coming back to it all evening. The theme was always the same. Ned wasn't a coward. He couldn't have done what they said.

Georgia hadn't had the heart to try and burst her

grandmother's optimism, which was why she was crossing the bridge at Breech's Inlet the next day, on her way to Isle of Palms to pick up the enhanced photos from Adam.

She headed down Palm Boulevard, glancing at the new houses that lined the road. Much of Isle of Palms had been rebuilt after Hurricane Hugo, giving it a newer look than Sullivan's Island.

She'd called Amanda before she left, hoping that she'd come up with something, but the news had all been negative. Whatever Ned had done back in 1942, it hadn't made the local papers.

She turned onto the side street where Adam rented a house with three of his Coast Guard buddies. Running perpendicular to the coastline, the short street ended at the beach. When Adam wasn't out on the water, he still wanted to be near it.

Her heart sank as she pulled up in front of the tan bungalow. Her mother's car was in the driveway.

She should not feel this way. Mamma meant well. But after the disappointment she'd shown at the news of Georgia's broken engagement, Georgia had been just as glad to avoid further conversation on that topic.

She couldn't hide forever. She slid out of the car and marched to the door.

Giving a cursory knock, she opened it and stepped inside, meeting the gazes of the two people in the room.

"Georgia Lee, at last." Mamma enveloped her in a Chanel-scented hug, kissing the air near her cheek. "I was beginnin' to think you'd forgotten you have other family besides Miz Callie."

Georgia sent an accusing look toward Adam, but he shrugged helplessly, as if denying he'd set this up.

"Mamma, you did bring me home to help Miz Callie, remember?"

"To help us reason with Miz Callie," her mother corrected. "How are you coming with that?"

Georgia took a step back, thinking fast. "I'm making a little progress, I guess." Mamma didn't need to know exactly what she was making progress on, did she?

"Good, good." Her mother glanced from her to Adam. "What are the two of you up to?"

"Nothing," she said quickly, reminded of answering that question in exactly the same way a few hundred times while growing up.

"Miz Callie had some old photographs she wanted me to work on," Adam said easily. "Georgia dropped by to bug me about it." Adam could sound relaxed. After all, he wasn't hiding anything. "Hey, how about some sweet tea?"

"None for me, thanks," Mamma said. "I have a dozen errands to run, and I'd best get on with it."

"Georgia?"

"Yes, thanks." At least the subject of her broken

engagement hadn't come up, and if her mother was rushing out, she was safe.

Adam headed for the kitchen, and her mother turned to her, touching her cheek with a quick, light gesture.

"I've been wantin' to talk to you, sugar." The faintest frown showed briefly between her brows. "I wanted to say I'm sorry."

The apology was so unexpected that Georgia could only stare for a moment. "Sorry?" She found her voice. "For what?"

"I reacted badly when you told us about your engagement." She shook her head. "Why you didn't call me to begin with… Well, that doesn't matter," she said hurriedly. "You know I want you to be happy, don't you?"

Her throat was tight. "Yes, Mamma. I know."

Her mother blinked rapidly for an instant. "That's all right, then. I'm sure it will work out for the best." She glanced at the gold bracelet watch on her wrist that was a duplicate of the one Georgia wore— Christmas gifts from Dad. "Goodness, I must be going. You be good now, y'heah?"

With a quick wave, she hurried out the door, her mind already on to the next thing on her list.

"There, that wasn't so bad, was it?" Adam leaned against the door frame, grinning.

"Did you set that up?" she demanded.

"Not me." He tossed her a manila envelope.

"That's the best I could do with the photos. I'll get your tea."

She sank down on the leather couch, opened the envelope and let the photos slide out onto her lap. When Adam returned, a glass in each hand, she looked up at him in amazement.

"These are wonderful. I had no idea you could do so much with your photo software."

"Black and whites are a lot easier than color." He leaned over her, looking at the pictures. "You think Miz Callie will be happy?"

"She'll be delighted. You just might move into the favorite grandchild spot."

"That'll be the day." The laughter in his eyes became muted. "Hey, it's better between you and Mamma, isn't it? She's trying."

"I know. Mamma will support me because she loves me." She managed a smile. "I just can't help wishing she'd support me because I'm right."

He shrugged. "I don't guess we can change the folks at this point. Mamma was raised to believe daughters got married." He eyed her. "'Course, you could still satisfy her on that."

She felt a betraying flush come up in her cheeks. "I don't know what you mean."

"Seems like you've been spending a lot of time with Matthew Harper." His eyes twinkled. "Can't be all business, can it?" He threw his arm over her shoulder in a hug. "Come on. Tell your big brother."

She leaned against him. "It's complicated."

"It always is."

She shoved him gently. "You should talk. You've never been serious about a woman for more than six weeks."

"You're the serious type, Little Bit." The humor left his eyes, replaced by concern. "Don't talk about it if you don't want to. Just don't get hurt."

"I'll try not to." But that might be out of her control.

Matt had been a little uncomfortable when Miz Callie called with an invitation to come for dessert and to discuss what she'd gleaned from the photographs. But now that he and Lindsay were sitting at the round table in Miz Callie's kitchen, finishing up slices of pecan pie topped with vanilla ice cream, he felt reassured.

Things were back to normal between him and Georgia. He'd been thrown off-balance earlier, but that wouldn't happen again. No more tête-à-têtes, no more exchanging confidences. Georgia was a client's granddaughter, helping him to fulfill a client's wishes.

And even as he thought these things, he knew he was kidding himself. Georgia could never be put into such a restrictive box, and what happened between them had been as inevitable as it was upsetting.

He glanced across the table as she rose and started to collect the dishes. Her hair was fastened at the nape of her neck with a silver clasp, and she wore a white sundress which looked…beautiful on her.

Enough, he ordered himself. "Wonderful pie, Miz Callie. Thanks for inviting us."

"It's our pleasure." Miz Callie glanced toward the living room, where he could see a sheaf of photos spread out on the coffee table. Her bright eyes betrayed her eagerness to get to the main reason for his visit.

Georgia cast a knowing eye at her grandmother and then turned to Lindsay. "I picked up a sketch-book and some drawing pencils for you today. Why don't we go on the deck and try them out?"

His daughter's eyes lit with almost as much enthusiasm as Miz Callie's. "Can we?" She jumped off her chair and then paused, as if caught in flight. "Thank you, Miz Callie. Daddy, may I be excused, please?"

He nodded. Georgia and Miz Callie had planned this to give them privacy to discuss the photos, but it was still a thoughtful act on Georgia's part.

Maybe thoughtful wasn't the right word. He watched her and Lindsay go out on the deck together, talking as easily as if they were the same age. That implied that she'd deliberately figured out what would please his daughter. Rather, she seemed to act instinctively.

He followed Miz Callie into the living room and took the seat she indicated next to her. She turned on the brass floor lamp, casting a pool of light on the table and the black-and-white photographs.

"I can't tell you how excited I am at the way these pictures turned out." Her fingers shook a little as she picked one up and handed it to him. "I had no idea Adam could do anything like this with that computer of his."

"Photo software is pretty sophisticated." He looked down at the picture. Young faces stared back at him, and he picked one out without any difficulty. "This is you, isn't it?"

She nodded. "I was about Lindsay's age then, I guess."

Like Lindsay, she'd been all arms and legs. Her hair was pulled back in a braid, and she wore that intent, impatient expression he sometimes caught on Lindsay's face, as if she'd been interrupted while doing something important.

He glanced through the sliding glass door at his daughter. She and Georgia sat side by side, both bending over their drawing pads.

"Lindsay has warmed up to Georgia now, hasn't she?"

"I guess so." He wasn't sure he wanted to discuss Georgia's relationship with his daughter.

Miz Callie, usually so perceptive, didn't seem to catch the reluctance in his voice. "They're good for each other. They have a lot in common. Georgia was feeling a bit lost when she came home."

He decided to ignore the implication that Lindsay was feeling lost. "I appreciate Georgia taking an interest in her."

"How formal." Miz Callie's eyes twinkled.

Embarrassed, he shook his head. "I didn't mean it that way." He hesitated, but the memory of Georgia's well-meant advice still rankled. "I don't suppose she knows a lot about young children."

"Georgia has a kind heart." Miz Callie's gaze rested fondly on her granddaughter. "I'll take that over book knowledge and degrees any day of the week."

He stiffened, but the last thing he wanted was to disagree with Miz Callie. "Maybe you're right," he said, his tone noncommittal.

Miz Callie was still watching Georgia. "I'm praying she'll decide to stay here, you know. She belongs here. I just hope she'll realize that."

What could he say? That he hoped she'd stay, too? He didn't have the right to hope anything of the kind, because it implied an interest he was determined not to have.

"About these pictures," he said.

"Yes, of course." Miz Callie turned back to the task at hand. "Just looking at them brings back so many memories. All these faces." She touched the picture he held, sighing a little. "We were all so young then."

Untouched by life. They'd had a privileged childhood that was as different as could be from his.

But for all the innocence in the faces, they couldn't have had an easy time of it. The older boys, Ned's contemporaries, were laughing and horsing around in one picture, but not long afterward, most of them were off to war. Even the younger children would have been affected, some with fathers gone for the duration. Or forever.

"There, now." Miz Callie put one photo down in front of him. "Those are Ned's particular friends."

Four boys in their late teens posed on a sailboat pulled up on the beach. Ned Bodine's face was familiar by now. He stood, hand resting against the mast, his air of unconscious pride telling clearly whose boat it was.

"This is Timothy Allen." She pointed to a suntanned blond boy who grinned up at Ned. "He died somewhere in Italy, I know." Her voice trembled.

"What about the other two? Do you remember their names?"

She nodded. "Phil Yancey and Bennett Adams."

"Did they survive the war?" That was the crucial question, if he was going to find someone who'd know what Ned Bodine was up to that summer.

"Yes, they did. I remember seeing them off and on over the years, but their families weren't really close to us. Just people who rented on the island that summer. I don't know where they are now."

He jotted down the names. "I'll find them." Assuming they were still alive to be found. "Anyone else?"

"Not anyone I think can help." Her hands, thin and deeply veined, moved over the photos. "Even so, I'm glad to have these to enjoy." She shook her head slightly, as if in wonderment. "Strange, but I just remember how happy we were. In spite of all the bad news from the war, and the shortages, and the worry on all the grown-ups' faces, we were still children, playing on the beach."

He was unaccountably touched. He wanted to say something that would let her know he understood, but before he could find the words, the door slid open.

"We finished our pictures," Georgia said as she and Lindsay came inside. "We decided to show them off."

"Look, Daddy. Look at my picture. Georgia showed me how to make the shell look round."

He took the sheet of drawing paper she thrust into his hands. "That's beautiful, Lindsay. I really like what you did with the colors, too."

She beamed, then snatched it from him to show Miz Callie. Georgia bent over them, the three heads close together as they talked about the drawing. Lindsay leaned unselfconsciously against Georgia.

As Miz Callie said, Lindsay was warming up to her. He should be happy to see that.

But what if Miz Callie was wrong about Georgia? What if Lindsay grew to count on her, and then Georgia flitted back to her life in Atlanta?

He stood, shoving his notebook into his pocket. "We have to go."

A questioning glance from Georgia told him that the words had come out too harshly.

"Daddy…" It was almost a wail from Lindsay.

"Sorry, Lindsay, but remember that your big Vacation Bible School program is tomorrow. You still have to practice your lines."

"Oh, right." She came to tug on his hand. "I want to make sure my costume is ready, too."

"Good night, sweet child." Miz Callie blew her a kiss.

"I'll walk out with you," Georgia said, sliding the door open again. A breeze flowed in, bringing with it the steady murmur of the ocean.

They'd reached the steps of the deck when Lindsay stopped.

"Daddy, I want to give my picture to Miz Callie. Can I?"

"Okay, run and do it."

She darted back inside, leaving him alone with Georgia for a moment.

"Any progress with Miz Callie?" she asked in a soft undertone.

"She gave me a couple of names that seem like good possibilities." He grasped the railing, turning back toward her. She was closer than he thought, and he caught a faint whiff of the fragrance she wore. "If she thinks of any other names, let me know."

"I will." She tilted her face to look up at him. The breeze lifted her hair and fluttered the hem of her dress. "Is something wrong? You seem in a hurry to leave."

"No, nothing." Nothing except that the longer he stood here, the less will he had to move away. The breeze seemed to be pressing him toward her. It tossed her hair capriciously, and a strand brushed his face, drawing him in closer. Closer.

Her eyes widened, and her lips parted on a breath. His fingers closed on her arms and he—

"I'm ready." Lindsay came clattering back onto the deck. "Miz Callie is going to hang my picture on the wall."

Georgia took a step back, turning to grasp the rail and stare out at the water.

Somehow he managed to find his breath. "That's great, Lindsay. Tell Georgia good-night, now."

"'Night, Georgia." Lindsay's voice trailed over her shoulder as she started down the steps.

He headed after her, taking them so fast it almost felt like flight. Almost? Who was he kidding? It was flight.

Chapter Twelve

Georgia took a load of clothes from the dryer and began folding, the chore a silent reminder that she must decide soon what she intended to do with her life.

Back in Atlanta she had an apartment, clothes and personal belongings, some good friends, no job and no fiancé. Here she had family, a set of friends from whom her life had been separate for too many years, no job, no apartment and a tentative relationship with Matthew that he'd backed away from so quickly it was a wonder he hadn't tripped. How did she make a pros-and-cons list out of that?

To be honest, she couldn't say she had no place to live. The peaceful silence of the beach house comforted her. Her grandmother would be delighted to have her stay as long as she wanted. Or she could move in with one of her cousins for a while.

Not home. She and her mother had made a positive step in their relationship yesterday, but she wouldn't kid herself. If she moved home, they'd fall right back into their old way of relating to each other.

As for Matt… That was a story that went nowhere.

The telephone rang, breaking off the futile line of thought. She hurried to answer it, since Miz Callie was off to spend the day with an old friend.

It was Matt, and he sounded a bit disconcerted when he realized she'd picked up. "Hi, Georgia… um, is Miz Callie there?"

"I'm sorry, but she's visiting a friend. Is there a message?" If Matt wanted to keep things strictly business between them, she'd show him that she could do that. Never mind that the sound of his deep voice in her ear did such funny things to her.

"No, no message." He sounded harried. "I wanted to ask a favor, but I'll find some other way to deal with it."

She paused for the briefest of seconds. "If there's something you need, just tell me." It was what her grandmother would say, what neighborliness demanded.

Now it was his turn to hesitate, and the phone line hummed with his unspoken thoughts.

"If you could help, I'd appreciate it. I'm stuck at the office. I can't possibly get away for another half hour, and the Bible school program will be starting soon. I promised Lindsay I'd be there."

She heard the frustration in his tone. He didn't want to let down his child. But he couldn't afford to walk out on a client.

"I'll go right over," she said. "Shall I tell Lindsay that you'll be coming as soon as you can?"

"Yes, please." Relief, so palpable she could almost touch it. "I don't want her to feel she doesn't have anyone to clap for her."

"No problem." She looked down in dismay at her faded T-shirt and oldest shorts. A quick change was in order. "I'm on my way."

A shower would be nice, but that was out of the question. She hit the stairs at a run. Luckily the church was only a few blocks away.

She reached the church with minutes to spare. Parents and grandparents were gathering in the fellowship hall, but the classes hadn't come in yet.

Following the signs, she made her way downstairs and hurried along the corridor. She couldn't let Lindsay walk into that big room and look in vain for her daddy.

She found the classroom, tapped on the door and opened it. The teacher was busily engaged in pinning what seemed to be butterfly wings onto the back of a little boy whose wiggling made it highly likely he'd end up on the pointed end of a pin.

"Georgia Bodine!" Grasping a chair, the woman levered herself to her feet and advanced on Georgia, arms spread wide. "It's great to see you."

"Candy, how are you?" Candy Morris had been in her grade all through school. She hugged her, then held her back. "You look wonderful."

"I look pregnant." Candy grinned and patted her belly. "Due in August, and I feel like a whale."

Georgia felt a pang of envy. "On you, it's beautiful."

A pair of arms clasped her around the waist. "Georgia, did you come to see me in the program?" Lindsay's eyes lit with pleasure.

"I sure did, sugar." She glanced at Candy. "Okay if I talk to Lindsay for a minute?"

"Of course. Then you can help me turn these young ones into birds and butterflies. If I'd known you were around, I'd have recruited you to help with more than that."

Candy turned back to her butterflies, and Georgia drew Lindsay aside, out of the turmoil.

"Is something the matter?" Lindsay's eyes filled with sudden fear. "Did my daddy have an accident?"

"No, no, certainly not." That must be the fear that lingered under the surface in the child's mind—that she would lose her father, too. How uncertain Lindsay's world must feel. "He wants me to tell you that he's on his way. He was delayed at the office for a bit, but he's coming." She brushed a strand of fine hair back from Lindsay's forehead. "Honest."

The child's eyes were wary, seeking confidence. "Okay," she said finally.

"His meeting went longer than it was supposed to." She'd probably already stressed too much that Matt would be here. If Lindsay were disappointed…well, she didn't want to think about that.

"Will you help me with my wings?" Lindsay slid her hand into Georgia's.

"I'd love to." Her heart expanded at the sign of trust. "Show me where they are."

She soon mastered the trick of pinning wings onto overexcited little bodies—just make sure that if the pin slips, you stab yourself.

Over a sea of jumping children, she raised an eyebrow at Candy. "Birds and butterflies?"

"We're doing the Creation story." Candy grinned. "Just be glad we didn't get the sun, moon and stars. Those costumes are tough."

Somewhere a bell rang, and she grabbed Georgia's hand. "Georgia, honey, my aide didn't show up today. Help me keep them in order while they wait to go on. Please?"

What did she know about managing groups of kids? Nothing. But she could hardly say no, so she nodded.

To her surprise, Candy had little difficulty in getting them lined up quietly, now that the time had arrived. Holding hands, the children walked in a line down the hall and up the stairs to the large room that had been turned into a temporary theater for the occasion.

A wave of nostalgia swept over Georgia. She remembered this. Vacation Bible School was a rite of childhood, and she'd always been thrilled when it rolled around. Thanks to her grandmother, she'd come to the one at this church as well as the one at her home church in Mount Pleasant.

Parents and grandparents sat in rows of metal folding chairs, cameras in evidence. At the end of the room nearest the kitchen, helpers buzzed around a table laden with refreshments for after the show. Fruit punch, she'd guess, and more kinds of cookies than anyone should possibly eat, although some of the kids would try. Some things didn't change.

Apparently awed by the audience, Candy's class stood quietly enough along the wall, watching as the youngest children sang songs. Georgia scanned the room. A number of people she knew were here, and she caught several looking at her. Wondering, maybe. *What's Miz Callie's granddaughter doing here? I thought she was working up in Atlanta.*

What was she doing here? Plenty of her classmates, like Candy, had settled down to marriage and family by now—their lives set in a familiar track. Not adrift like hers.

"We're next," Candy whispered. "You can sit and watch if you want. Thanks a million."

"My pleasure." She waved at Lindsay, and then skirted around the back of the audience to find a seat at the rear.

And there was Matt, slipping in the door just in time. She waved. He caught the motion, nodded and came to join her just as the birds and butterflies were introduced.

The program went on, as such things always did, with mistakes here and there that were easily forgiven by the audience. Each class performed to thunderous applause, and the finale led to a standing ovation.

She stood with the rest, clapping, feeling a surge of pride. She couldn't take credit for much, but she'd been there.

Lindsay raced through the crowd to hurl herself at her father. "Daddy, you got here!"

"I did." He bent, hugging her. "You were so good, sweetheart. I loved your song, and the motions were great."

"We were good, weren't we?" Lindsay did a little pirouette, beaming.

This was the most animated and outgoing Georgia had ever seen the child. Miz Callie had known what she was doing when she'd arranged for Lindsay to attend Vacation Bible School.

Matt straightened a butterfly wing. "It looks like a crush around the refreshments. Suppose I get drinks for all of us, so you don't get your wings ruined." His glance included Georgia.

"Red punch for me," Lindsay said.

"Anything but red punch for me."

"Right." Matt's face relaxed in a smile. "Thank you, Georgia. I owe you."

"It was a pleasure," she said, and meant it.

He began to work his way to the table. Lindsay, clinging to Georgia's hand, chattered away a mile a minute about the performance. "Someday I want to be thunder and lightning, like the big kids."

One of the older classes had produced some very effective weather effects with a metal sheet and some foam lightning bolts.

"You'll get to, when you're older." That was one of the pleasures of coming back year after year—working your way through the classes to play every part in the production.

"Next week I won't have anything to do." Lindsay drooped for a moment. "I wish Bible school wasn't over."

"There are lots of other fun things to do in the summer."

A woman with a daughter about Lindsay's age touched Georgia's arm. "Hi. I wanted to meet you. My Katie will be in the same grade as Lindsay when school starts. Maybe we can get our daughters together over the summer."

Georgia opened her mouth to correct the misconception, but she didn't get a chance. Lindsay did it for her.

"Don't say that!" The words rang out loudly in a sudden silence. "She's not my mother!"

Georgia tried for an apologetic smile and a light explanation, but as she sought the words, she saw Matt a few feet away, hands filled with paper cups, his face far more thunderous than anything the fifth and sixth graders had managed to produce.

He might as well have been hit in the stomach with a two-by-four. Matt stood, the drinks he held dripping on his fingers, fighting to regain control.

It wasn't just the assumption the woman had made. That was tough enough to deal with.

It was Lindsay's reaction that lent power to the punch. She hadn't said anything about her mother in so long that he'd begun to believe she'd moved past her grief.

Obviously she hadn't. How stupid could he get?

Georgia, smiling easily, set the woman straight. "I'm Lindsay's neighbor and friend, Georgia Bodine." She held out her hand.

The woman took it, flushing a little. "I'm so sorry. I didn't realize…" She stopped, started again. "I'm Linda Mulvaney. This is my daughter, Katie." Her flush deepened. "We're new on Sullivan's Island, you see. I was so pleased that Katie had made a friend her age."

Georgia, one hand resting lightly on Lindsay's shoulder, smiled at the other child. "It's nice to meet you, Katie. You're going to love Sullivan's Island Elementary School. It's really a fun place."

"Mommy says we'll go and visit soon." Katie tugged at her hand. "Do you think Lindsay could come to my house for a playdate?"

"I'll bet your mom could arrange that with Lindsay's dad." She nodded toward him, then came and took the cups from his hands. "Linda Mulvaney, this is Matthew Harper."

With half his mind caught up in worrying about his daughter, he fought to speak coherently to the woman. "I'm sure Lindsay would love to get together with Katie. Why don't I give you my number?" He pulled out his card.

"That's great." She tucked it into her bag. "Again, I'm sorry about the misunderstanding."

"Don't be, please. How could you know?" Even as he reassured the woman, he eyed his daughter, nerves jangling.

Georgia bent over Lindsay, talking to her earnestly. Whatever she was saying seemed to wipe the strain from his daughter's face.

Mrs. Mulvaney's attention was distracted by another mother, and she moved off. Georgia gestured toward a pair of folding chairs, and Katie and Lindsay sat down, their legs swinging in unison, heads together.

"It's great that Lindsay made a friend," Georgia said cautiously to Matt.

"She seems okay now. What did you say to her?"

"I just explained that Katie's mother didn't know

us. That it was a mistake, easily fixed." She gazed at him, concern plain in her eyes. "I'm sorry if her comment upset you."

"It didn't." He wasn't being honest, and he suspected Georgia knew that. The incident had bothered him, upsetting his precarious view of how things were. "Katie's mother is going to call me so we can set a time to get the girls together."

"Life was simpler when I was a kid. Our neighborhood in Mount Pleasant had kids in every house. All you had to do to make a friend was go out the front door. Now the parents have to get involved."

"Jennifer used to do that. Even before Lindsay started school, she'd organized a playgroup for her." Jennifer had been so intent on doing everything right when it came to raising their daughter. "I should have picked up on that."

"It's tough in a new place." Georgia's voice was warm with sympathy. "Now that Lindsay has one friend, she'll meet others. By the time school starts, she'll have a group of girls to hang around with."

That would have been what Georgia's life was like at eight. A nice house in a nice neighborhood, lots of friends. He had no basis for comparison. But his daughter would. He'd make sure of it.

"I should have seen it sooner." His gaze fixed on his daughter. "I should have realized that she needed help making friends."

She patted his arm lightly, sympathy flowing

through her very touch. "You've had plenty to deal with. If you'd stayed in Boston…" She let that trail off, as if she didn't want to go there.

"If we'd stayed in Boston, we'd have had friends to support us." He took a breath, remembering what it had been like. "But Lindsay couldn't deal with that. Neither could I. Maybe the two of us are more alike than I thought."

"It bothered you, being with friends whose families were still intact." She seemed to understand without questions.

"It did." He glanced around, but no one was close enough to hear. "We were rattling around in that house together, looking for Jennifer around every corner." His voice thickened. "The grief was everywhere. I felt as if we were both drowning in it."

"So you decided to make a fresh start here."

"Yes." His throat was tight. "I guess I thought we could outrun our grief, but I was wrong. We can't."

And now he'd complicated everything by showing Georgia the depth of his emotional failings. He hated not being in control of his feelings. He'd thought he could get over his grief, help Lindsay get over her grief, by starting fresh.

Guilt flooded him. He'd been disloyal, trying to escape the fact of Jennifer's death. Then doubly disloyal for having feelings for Georgia.

Wouldn't Jennifer want him to love again? The

thought, coming out of nowhere, was like a punch in the heart. For an instant he was numb. The anger rushed in. It wasn't fair. None of this was fair.

Chapter Thirteen

After yesterday's revelation, Georgia hadn't been sure how Matt would react to her today. But he'd picked her up right on time, and a glance had assured her that he had his game face on.

"Are you sure that this man understood why we want to talk with him?" Matt had already located one of the two men Miz Callie had identified, living just a few minutes' drive away in North Charleston. "He must be getting up in years."

"In his eighties, but very much all there, from what I could tell." Matt smiled. "We had to come this morning, because he has a bocce-ball tournament this afternoon."

Georgia glanced down at the Ashley River far below as they drove across the bridge. "That does sound pretty lively."

"He may not know anything, but it's worth the effort."

He was right. So far they had absolutely nothing. Even Miz Callie's hope had begun to dim a little, she thought. She was losing her faith that they'd ever find evidence to exonerate Ned.

She glanced at Matt, but his face didn't give anything away. She longed to speak to him again about Lindsay. Even an amateur like her could see that the child needed help with her grief.

Steeling herself for his reaction, she took a breath. "I want to talk to you again about Lindsay."

He shot her a look that threatened to pin her back against the car door. "I don't—"

"About her birthday," she said quickly, her courage failing. "Miz Callie would like to have a little party for her. They were talking about a crab boil on the beach, and Lindsay was intrigued. So Miz Callie thought we could do that, unless you have other plans."

His face relaxed. "That's very kind of her, but isn't it too much trouble? I don't want her wearing herself out for Lindsay."

"I don't think she's ever gotten tired from planning a party. It's one of her favorite things. When we were little, she loved having our parties on the island. She put on a treasure hunt for my ninth birthday that I still remember."

"Only if she'll let me buy the supplies and help with the work."

She grinned. "You can try arguing with her

over that, but I wouldn't make a bet on your winning."

"It's only fair—" he began.

"She loves Lindsay. She wants to do something nice for her. Besides, it'll distract her from the information we don't have."

"You have a point there." His brows drew down. "The paperwork is moving along a lot faster than I expected. You know, the further this goes, the more likely it is that Miz Callie's plans will get out."

She nodded, not liking the sense that time was working against them. "Can't you slow it down a bit?"

"I'd have to reckon with your grandmother if I did that." Matt's navigation system beeped, and he turned onto the street they wanted. "Let's just hope Bennett Adams has something to say."

She leaned forward, watching the house numbers. "If he did, you'd think he'd have come out with it before this."

The navigation system announced their arrival just as Georgia pointed to the house, and Matt pulled to the curb. "There could be a lot of reasons why he'd keep quiet," he said. "We'll just have to play it by ear."

They got out of the car. As they started up the flagstone walk toward the small cottage, Matt's hand was at her back. She felt its warmth right through her.

The front door swung open at their approach. "Hey, there. Welcome. Y'all come in now."

Bennett Adams was tiny, barely taller than Georgia. Bald and a bit frail-looking, he had snapping brown eyes that were full of life.

"Mr. Adams, I'm Matt Harper." Matt extended his hand. "And this is Georgia Bodine."

"Call me Benny. So you're Georgia." He took her hand, holding it for a long moment. "Little Callie's granddaughter. You have the look of her, you know."

"I hope so." She warmed to him at once. Like Miz Callie, Adams seemed to be the kind of person who didn't let age keep him from enjoying life.

"Come and sit down." He waved his hand toward a sofa in front of the window of the crowded, minuscule living room. He sat in a threadbare recliner and leaned forward, elbows on his knees. "So what's this all about, then?"

"Miz Callie is living out at the Sullivan's Island house now, the one that belonged to the Bodines. Do you remember it?"

"'Course I do. The Bodines pretty much held open house for their kids' friends during the summer, even during the war years."

"My grandmother has been thinking a lot about that time, especially the summer of 1942." She took a breath and plunged ahead. "She wants to find out what happened to her husband's older brother, Ned Bodine."

His eyes grew guarded at the name. "Seems way too late for that, don't it?"

Georgia leaned forward, hands clasped. "She's desperate to do this. She believes Ned has been treated unjustly all these years—that he'd never have run away rather than join up. Please, if you know anything, tell us."

"I don't know what happened to him when he went away, if that's what you mean." He shook his head. "I'm right sorry to let little Callie down, but I don't know."

Her heart sank. That was it, then.

"You were on the island when he disappeared," Matt said. "Anything you can remember about Ned might help."

"I don't see how." He leaned back, as if retreating from them.

"Please." She extended a hand, palm up, asking.

He shrugged. Shook his head. "I do remember he fought with his father all that summer about enlisting," Benny said slowly. "Funny, that was. All any of us boys could talk about was how we were going to enlist, minute we were old enough."

"Ned didn't feel that way?" Matt put the question quietly.

"At first he did. Beginning of the summer, we made a pact that we'd go enlist together. Our birthdays were only a couple days apart, you see."

"But that changed?"

He nodded. "That was what all the fighting with his daddy was about. Seemed like Ned was changing his mind, delaying in a way. Old Mr. Bodine was a real fire-eater. He'd have gone off to fight himself if they'd have taken him."

"Do you know why Ned changed his mind?"

"Not because he was scared, if that's what you're thinking." Brown eyes locked on to them. "Mind, Ned wasn't foolish daring, like some of us were, but he never backed away from anything or anybody."

"Then why did he change his mind about enlisting?"

Benny's gaze slid away, and he picked at a loose thread on the arm of the recliner. "Don't know as I know. I wouldn't want to guess."

She exchanged a look with Matt. The man knew something. Whether they could get it out of him…

Matt nodded, as if telling her to pursue it, probably thinking the man was more likely to tell her. He had good insight into what made people tick—no doubt an asset to an attorney.

"Mr. Adams—Benny, please. If you know something, even guess something, please tell us. My grandmother is so set on finding out the truth. It will hurt her terribly to never know. And hurt me, too, if I can't do this thing for her."

"Well, now, young lady, you know how to make it hard on a person. If I had a granddaughter like you…" He shook his head. "Suppose I told you something about Ned that…well, some folks might think was a slur on his character. Don't you think your grandmother would rather remember him the way she does?"

She straightened. "If you still knew Callie Bodine, you wouldn't ask that. She'd rather have the truth, every time."

He studied her face for a long moment, as if assessing her determination. Finally he nodded.

"All right then. I'll tell you what I thought, but mind, Ned never confided in me about it. I'm just saying what I thought."

Her fingers twined tightly. Were they finally going to get some insight? She could sense Matt's tension, his yearning to find answers at last.

Benny frowned, gazing back into the past. "There was a couple from Charleston rented a place out on the island that summer. Can't say anybody really took to him—big, blustery kind of guy, wore flashy clothes and talked loud all the time. Gossip said he was into the black market, but I don't know if that was true."

He surely wasn't going to imply that Ned was involved in anything like that—was he?

"Now, his wife was something different altogether. A lady. Pretty, too. Why she wanted to take up with a fella like that, nobody could figure." He shook his head. "It wasn't a very happy marriage, by all accounts." He stopped, as if reluctant to go on.

"Please…"

"You're thinking Ned was involved with the wife," Matt said, quicker than she was to reach the conclusion.

"I'm not saying that." He held up his hands in denial. "But she was an awful pretty woman. She'd be out on the beach lots of times when us kids were out, and seemed like she enjoyed our company."

"How did Ned react?" Matt asked.

Benny shrugged. "Didn't talk about it much. I remember one time when the husband had been drinking too much and making a fool of himself, Ned said that it was a pity with all the good men getting killed, a skunk like that was still walking around."

"Do you remember what their name was?" She held her breath, hoping they weren't going to have to track down every summer visitor to the island in 1942.

He frowned. "Malloy, that was it. Don't recall first names, but the last name was Malloy."

"Do you know which house they rented?" Some of the rental agents could have records.

"It's not there anymore, is it?" He shook his head, as if regretting all that was gone. "Tore it down like they did a lot of places, but it was the second place down island from the Bodine house. That's how we come to see her on the beach so often, you see."

He shook his head, some of the spirit seeming to go out of him. "Ah, it's a long time ago now. We were all close as could be that summer, but come Labor Day, folks started to leave. I enlisted—infantry. Got over to Europe in time to do my share. Most of those folks I lost track of by the time I finally come home again. You know how it is."

She didn't, but she could imagine. The world had been turned upside down, and they'd all been part of it.

"Thank you." She took his hand, clasping it firmly in hers. "I can't tell you how much it means to me to hear your story."

He put his other hand over hers. "Mind, I can't say anything for sure. It's just my idea of what was going on."

"I know." She rose, bending to kiss his cheek.

He flushed. "I hope it does some good."

Matt shook his hand. "Thanks for letting us impose on you this morning."

"Impose nothing." He rose to walk with them to the door. "It's rare enough when I get company, and even rarer when somebody wants to talk about the old days. Now, you give my respects to your grandmother, y'heah?"

"I will. I'm sure she'll be grateful, too."

But doubt assailed her as they stepped off the narrow porch. She glanced up at Matt. "At least, she will if we tell her."

He lifted an eyebrow. "Afraid Miz Callie wouldn't like having her hero's image clouded?"

"I don't know. Maybe."

He opened the gate, holding it for her. "Miz Callie always struck me as being wise in the ways of the heart. I doubt she's going to be shocked by this."

She thought of her grandmother's calm comfort over her broken engagement. "Maybe you're right."

Matt squeezed her hand. "Don't worry so much. Miz Callie wants the truth, no matter where it takes us."

She managed a nod, despite the fact that she felt as if he'd squeezed her heart instead of her hand. A wave of panic swept through her. She was getting in way over her head with Matt. What would Miz Callie have to say about that?

"Exactly how many people have you invited to this party?" Georgia paused while cutting up cantaloupe for the fruit salad, assessing the size of the bowl—Miz Callie's largest, she felt sure.

Her grandmother evaded her gaze. "Oh, I don't know exactly. Folks just hear about it. You know how it is."

She did indeed know how it was. Miz Callie's beach parties always started out small. They never ended up that way. An unpleasant sensation crawled across her skin at the memory of how one particular crab boil had ended up.

"Does it still bother you?" Miz Callie, exhibiting

her uncanny ability to read one's thoughts through the smallest reaction, stopped stirring a pitcher of lemonade to cast a look of concern at Georgia. "What happened with Cole's roommate, I mean."

"No, of course not." She forced a smile she didn't feel. "I didn't even think you knew. How silly would that be, to brood about something that happened ages ago?"

She didn't think Miz Callie bought that, but she didn't push, either, thank goodness.

Georgia didn't want to remember that incident. She'd been young for her years, inexperienced, and she'd acted like an idiot. End of story.

"If you think the crowd is going to be bigger than expected, maybe I ought to pick up more crabs and shrimp." She looked down at her fruit-stained T-shirt. "But I'd have to change clothes first."

"No need," she said. "Adam's taking care of it."

"Adam. As in my brother Adam? But he doesn't even know Lindsay."

"Well, now he will." Miz Callie shut the refrigerator door firmly on the lemonade.

A sinking feeling gripped her stomach. "Just how many Bodines are going to show up tonight?"

"Anybody who wants to. Now, Georgia, you stop worrying. Things are going to turn out fine. Look how much progress you and Matt have made already."

She wasn't sure she'd define what they found out

as progress. On Sunday, sitting in the simple, airy sanctuary of the church Ned must have attended, she'd found herself wondering what it would have been like for him. Had he looked up at the plain wooden cross and wrestled with God over his feelings for a married woman? Had he begged for forgiveness and then run away with her?

"Matt's trying to trace the woman, but I don't know how easy it will be." She hesitated, not sure she should bring up the thing that bothered her most. But someone had to. "Suppose we do find her. Suppose we find that Ned left everything behind—his family, his duty—and ran off with her. Can you forgive that?"

The sorrow in Miz Callie's eyes told Georgia that she had already considered that. "Forgiveness wouldn't be up to me. That would be between Ned and God."

"I know. But…" She frowned down at the bowl of fruit and tried to find the words to express what she felt. "When you let somebody love you, it seems to me you become responsible. You can't turn your back on them without hurting them and losing a little bit of yourself."

That was as good an explanation as any for what had been wrong between her and James. He'd turned his back on her, and it hadn't, as far as she could tell, cost him anything. His heart had remained perfectly intact, which must mean that it hadn't been engaged at all.

"You have something there." Her grandmother's voice was soft. "Love costs. How did you get so smart?"

She smiled, despite the tears that stung her eyes. "From watching my grandmother."

Miz Callie shook her head. "Took me a lot longer to figure out how people work, it seems to me. But I know that forgiveness isn't up to us. We've all done things—" She stopped suddenly, hands tightening around a dish towel, staring out the window at the dunes.

"What's wrong?" Georgia peered through the window, seeing nothing unusual.

Miz Callie planted her hands on the table. "We were talkin', and all of a sudden it was like a door opened in my mind and a memory fell out."

"A memory of what?" For a moment she'd been alarmed, but Miz Callie seemed all right. It was what Aunt Lizbet had said, too, when a memory from the distant past emerged.

"Your granddad and I, out way later than we should have been, I'm sure, 'cause it was already getting dark. Enough moonlight to see where we were going, though, and Richmond—well, he could have found his way home blindfolded from anywhere on the island. We were coming by one of the cottages, and we could hear somebody inside." She shivered, as if she were that child again, standing out in the dunes on a summer night. "Not that we never heard folks yelling—our folks yelled at us when we needed it. But this was different—a man's voice, mean. We stood there, holding hands, scared and not knowing what to do. And then there was the sound of a slap, and a woman crying."

Georgia didn't need to ask whose house it had been. It fit only too clearly with what Benny had said.

Miz Callie's hand was extended, as if she still clasped the hand of her Richmond. "Then we saw we weren't alone. Ned stood there in the dunes, stiff as a statue, staring at that house. Only thing that moved was his hands, working like he wanted to tear something. I'd never seen him like that—never even dreamed he could look that way."

Miz Callie stopped, seeming stuck at that image. "Did he see you?"

"He did, and then he was himself again. Told us to cut along home. Richmond wanted him to come with us, but he said he wasn't ready to go in yet." She rubbed her hands on her apron. "Funny. I thought we'd ask him about what happened. Ned was good at explaining things grown-ups might not want to talk about. But Richmond said better not, so we never did. Guess it doesn't mean much."

Georgia wouldn't soon get that image out of her mind of a young Ned, standing out in the dunes, unable to help the woman he loved.

Love costs, Miz Callie had said. What had it cost Ned?

"Miz Callie! Georgia! I'm here. Can I help?"

Lindsay slid the glass door back and burst into the kitchen, shattering the silence.

"If it isn't the birthday girl." Miz Callie grabbed her and kissed her. "You best get used to being kissed, child, 'cause we give lots of kisses on your birthday."

"I'm eight. That's getting pretty grown-up, isn't it?" She came to Georgia, lifting her face for a kiss.

Georgia kissed her and held her close for a moment. "Almost old enough to vote," she said. "Happy birthday, sugar. Where's your daddy?"

"He's on the beach, helping the men. What can I do?"

On the beach, helping the men. What men? Georgia stepped out to the deck and looked down. She spotted Matt instantly among the group stacking driftwood for a fire. Matt was being exposed to way too many Bodine males at once— her father, Adam, a couple of cousins—and there wasn't a thing she could do to help him.

She turned back to Lindsay. Maybe she and Lindsay should go out and dilute all that testosterone.

"How about if you help me carry things out, okay?"

"Okay." Lindsay danced in place while Georgia loaded a basket for her with paper plates, napkins and cups. "Did you know that a bunch of my friends from Bible school are going to be here? And Miz Candy, my teacher, too."

"That'll be great." Georgia grabbed a roll of plastic tablecover, scissors and tape, and a thermos of sweet tea. "Okay, let's go."

Lindsay hurried out ahead of her, but her steps slowed as she started down toward the dunes. Georgia caught up with her, and they went side by side.

"Last year I had a party at the bouncy place," she said. "And the year before at the gym."

"I'll bet those were fun," Georgia said, noticing the sudden frown on Lindsay's face.

"They were." She emphasized the words. "My mommy did them, and she invited all my friends and decorated and had my favorite kind of cake and pizza and everything."

Georgia's heart twisted. Poor child. She felt disloyal enjoying a party that was so different from what her mother would have done.

She fought to keep emotion out of her voice. "Your mommy gave you really special parties."

Lindsay nodded.

"This year Daddy and Miz Callie are giving you an island-girl party, because you're an island girl now. That's different, but it's okay to like different things."

Lindsay didn't say anything for a moment.

Had she said the right thing? *Don't let me make*

a mistake when it comes to this child, Lord. She's had too many hurts already.

She'd been praying for Lindsay since the day they'd met, but a little extra prayer for help never went amiss.

They reached the beach, and Lindsay ran ahead to Matt. "I'm having an island-girl party this year," she said. "It's okay to like different kinds of parties."

Matt's gaze caught hers and held warmly for a moment. Then he turned back to his daughter.

"That's exactly right, Lindsay. It's just fine."

"What's not to like about any kind of party?" Georgia's cousin Win threw an arm around her waist and lifted her off her feet in a hug. "Hey, G, how come you haven't been out here helping with the work?"

"Put me down, you idiot." Georgia swatted at him. "Matt, Lindsay, this is my cousin Win Bodine. Win's a rescue swimmer, so he has to show off how strong he is."

Lindsay looked up at him solemnly. "Is your name really Win?"

He bent to shake her hand. "It's really Winthrop Richmond Bodine, but that's too big a mouthful, sugar, so you just call me Win."

Lindsay responded to the honey in Win's voice like women of every age seemed to, the corners of her lips curling up. "What's a rescue swimmer?"

Win, bless him, showed no sign of impatience with her questions. "That's just my job, darlin'."

"He jumps out of helicopters instead of piloting a cutter like any self-respecting Bodine ought to," Adam put in. He gave Win a cousinly shove. "Go say hi to Matt and let me talk to the birthday girl for a minute."

Georgia kept a watchful eye on Win as he approached Matt, but he seemed to be on his best behavior. Adam led Lindsay off to help him find some driftwood. Daddy, on his way toward her, paused to wave at folks coming down the path from the cottage. The beach party had begun—for better or worse.

Chapter Fourteen

Matt leaned back on his elbows, watching the fire as it burned lower. The party was slowly winding down. The sun had slid from sight, painting the fair-weather clouds on the horizon in shades that began as iridescent pink and faded to pale lilac and deep purple.

Across from him, Win Bodine reached forward to throw another piece of driftwood on the fire, sending sparks showering upward. Maybe he, too, hated to see this perfect evening come to an end.

The families with young children had been the first to go, trudging toward the road or down the beach with protesting youngsters in tow. But by then, he'd had the satisfying sense that Lindsay now had friends and acceptance here.

Thanks to the Bodines. Whether intentional or not, he and Lindsay were now associated with the Bodine family in people's minds.

A faint unease touched him. That could blow up in his face, depending on how things worked out with Miz Callie's plan.

Another shower of sparks flew up, casting light on those who surrounded the fire. Lindsay was curled on a blanket next to Miz Callie, and it looked as if the older woman was telling her a story. Across from him, Georgia's father was deep in conversation with her uncle Brett, while Adam and Win threw in an occasional comment. He didn't have the Bodine family tree worked out yet, but he thought Win was the son of Harrison, the brother he had yet to meet.

Amanda was telling some anecdote, complete with extravagant gestures, to her mother, her aunt and another young woman who'd been introduced as Amanda's twin. Georgia worked her way around the fire, offering coffee.

He probably should make a move toward home, but no one seemed in any hurry. Lindsay was content, so he lingered, enjoying watching the Bodines in their natural habitat.

From what he'd observed, Bodines, especially the males, came in a couple of distinct types. Georgia's father, for instance, was deliberate, calm, slow to speak and probably slow to anger as well. Adam was like him in temperament, listening with a wry smile to something his impassioned cousin was telling him.

Win was another kettle of fish altogether. Volatile, quick, probably daring or even reckless—the type who'd flare up in an instant. Georgia's uncle had shown him that side as well in their private encounter.

"Coffee?" Georgia leaned over him, coffee pot poised.

"I couldn't put another thing in my stomach." He patted the blanket beside him. "Can't you sit down and relax?"

"I can." She sank bonelessly into a cross-legged seat, her gaze moving from face to face. "I love this part of the evening. I used to be curled up on the blanket next to Miz Callie like Lindsay is." She smiled. "The voices were like sweet music, lulling me to sleep."

He could almost imagine a childhood like that. "I don't know how to thank you for doing this—"

She cut him off with a wave of her hand. "Miz Callie loved every minute of it. As for the rest of them—well, they love any excuse for a beach party, and giving Lindsay a happy birthday was a good one."

A soft outburst of laughter came from the women across the fire, and Win leaned forward, saying something that brought another ripple of laughter.

Georgia leaned closer to him. "What are you thinking about? You've been watching my kinfolk the way Miz Callie watches the turtles. Learning about a different species?"

"Something like that. I'm intrigued by how the Bodines seem to fall into two distinct personality types. Makes you believe in the power of genetics."

Georgia laughed. "You've exposed the Bodine family secret, though I wonder sometimes if it's not a case of living up to expectations. Adam—"

"Calm, fair, evenhanded," he put in.

"Like my daddy, and his daddy before him. And Win is just like Uncle Brett."

"Quick-tempered?"

She nodded. "But good-hearted and generous to a fault."

"What about your brother Cole? Is he the quick-tempered one of your family?"

She glanced away from him. "You could say that," she said, her voice barely audible.

"Georgia?" He touched her hand, smoothing his fingers over hers. "Did I say something wrong?"

She shook her head, managing a low laugh that didn't sound very amused. "Sorry. It's silly. Your comment about Cole just reminded me of something."

He shouldn't pry, but instinct stronger than common sense drove him. "Tell me." They were very close, their voices so soft they were in a small world of their own.

Her breath came out in a sigh. "It was stupid. Not my proudest moment, believe me."

Where was this leading? Whatever it was, it obviously hurt more than she wanted to show.

"I can't believe you did anything that stupid." It was something to do with her brother, obviously. "Cole lost his temper with you?"

"Not with me," she said quickly. She shook her head. "I'm making this sound worse than it is. It's just—nothing really."

He waited. She wanted, or needed, to say this tonight. He could feel the pressure inside her.

"Cole was at the Citadel then. I was a senior in high school. He brought his roommate home for the weekend, and we entertained him with a crab boil on the beach."

Her hand twisted a little in his—the only outward sign of her inward perturbation. "He acted—well, interested in me. I was flattered. None of Cole's friends had ever seen me as anything other than a little sister."

Now he thought he saw where this was going.

"Anyway, to make a long story short, he got carried away, and I didn't know how to handle it. That was the stupid part. Any other girl my age probably could have cut the thing short before it escalated...."

She stopped, her breath catching. He felt a totally irrational urge to find that unknown jerk and show him what you learned growing up on the streets of Boston.

"I take it Cole flew to your defense." He made an effort to keep his voice calm. It wouldn't do her any good if he overreacted to a ten-year-old trauma.

She nodded. "They had to pull him off the boy. He got into trouble at school as well, since that's not the kind of behavior the Citadel expects from its cadets." She tried to smile and failed. "All because I didn't know how to handle—"

"Don't." He couldn't help it—he had to touch her lips to stop her. Aware of her parents across the fire, he took his hand away quickly. "It wasn't your fault. And if Cole was here, I'd shake his hand right now."

That earned a shaky smile from her. "The last thing he needs is encouragement. Daddy rarely gets angry, but that time was the exception. And Mamma pointed out that if I'd shown a bit of maturity, it never would have happened."

The depth of empathy he felt for her shocked him. It probably wasn't a good idea to say what he thought of her mother's response.

"Georgia—"

"Daddy!" Lindsay's voice was almost a wail. "I can't find my new stuffed turtle that Georgia gave me."

"It's right here, sugar." Georgia was on her feet even faster than he was. "I put it in this shopping bag so it'd be easier to carry home."

Lindsay nuzzled the toy sleepily. "I want him to go to bed with me tonight."

"Sure you do. And we should be heading in that direction already." He stood and went to her.

"But I don't want to go home. I don't want my

beautiful party to be over." Her voice hinted at tears not far away.

He heard a murmur of empathy and a soft "Bless her heart" from someone.

"Nobody ever wants a beautiful day to end," Miz Callie said quietly but with a firm note in her voice that he suspected most eight-year-olds would heed. "But the stars are in their places, and all the little beach creatures are in their sandy beds. It's time you were as well."

"I want Georgia to walk us home." Lindsay grabbed Georgia's hand. "Please."

"Sure thing." She picked up one of the gift bags. "I'll help you carry all your loot home, birthday girl."

He bent over Miz Callie. "Thank you isn't enough." He kissed her cheek.

"It's more than enough," she said. "Bless you, dear."

He'd better go before he showed how much that meant to him. He picked up the rest of their belongings, and they started off down the beach to a chorus of good-nights.

Georgia, holding Lindsay's hand, was jollying her along, averting a meltdown better than he would have. That gave him a few minutes to digest what Georgia had told him. The incident had hurt her, and she'd been made to feel it was her fault. Oh, probably no one had intended that. He was even willing to give her mother the benefit of the doubt now that his temper had cooled a bit.

But they had handled it wrong, and Georgia had been the loser. The fact that the story had bubbled to the surface after all this time showed that she hadn't really resolved it.

His hands clenched again at the thought of that testosterone-laden teenager. Hopefully Cole had landed a few good punches before they'd pulled him off.

That did no good, he reminded himself. He should have said—well, he didn't know what he should have said, but he knew he couldn't leave it alone yet.

They'd reached the house, and he pulled out the key to unlock the door.

"I'll help you get things inside, and then I'll be off," Georgia said.

"Wait a minute, please." He touched Lindsay's shoulder. "You go on and slip into your pajamas, Lindsay. I need to tell Georgia something."

Lindsay was too sleepy to argue. Clutching the stuffed turtle, she headed for her room.

His hand on the curve of Georgia's back, he led her to the deck. Her face was a smooth, ivory oval in the moonlight.

"What is it?"

"Just something I didn't have the wit to say earlier. You were putting yourself down for not being able to handle a guy who was older, bigger, stronger and probably very determined. That's nonsense."

"If it had been Amanda, she'd have let him know—"

He put his fingers on her lips to stop her. This time her parents weren't sitting across from them. This time he didn't take them away.

"Don't. Don't compare yourself to your cousin. I'm sure she's a very admirable person—"

Her lips curved in a smile against his fingers. "She is."

"But she's not you." His fingers moved from her lips, caressing her cheek. "Don't you know how valuable you are? You're warmhearted, loving, filled with integrity. That's Georgia, no one else."

Her eyes sparkled in the moonlight, as if with tears. "That's the kind of thing Miz Callie would say. She always says that God created each one of us unique."

"Your grandmother is a wise woman." His heart seemed to be yearning toward the faith he'd once felt was so strong. "I can't pretend to be as wise as she is, but I try to believe that God has a purpose for who we are and a role we're meant to fill."

His own words startled him. How often had he stopped to ask if he was filling the role God had for him?

"So God needs an Amanda for one destiny, and

he gives her the gifts she needs to fulfill that." She seemed to be turning it over in her mind.

"And He's created you for a role only you can fill."

"I just have to find it." She was taking his words seriously, and that moved him.

"Yes." He wanted to say more, but his feelings were too near the surface.

"Thank you, Matt." She spoke softly, her voice a murmur on the breeze. "I'm glad we talked."

"I am, too."

She'd told him something he suspected she'd told very few other people. He was honored—and scared. They were dangerously close in the moonlight, and his hand cradled the smooth, soft line of her cheek.

"Daddy," Lindsay called from upstairs. "I'm ready."

"I should go." But she didn't move.

Neither did he. And then his lips found hers in a kiss that seemed irrevocable. His fingers raked back through her curls so that he held the back of her head, her hair twining around his hand as if to hold him fast.

Every cell in his body was aware of her. A wave of tenderness swept through him, mixed with longing. He should end this, but he couldn't.

She did it for him. She moved, taking a step back. Her fingers touched her lips and her breath was uneven.

"Lindsay wants you." Her smile trembled. "Good night, Matt."

He should go to Lindsay. He would, but he stood watching first as Georgia went swiftly down the steps.

When Matt pulled up at the cottage the next day, Georgia hurried down the stairs, holding an umbrella to ward off the rain that had started during the night.

She was trying to ignore the fluttering in the pit of her stomach, trying to tell herself she felt that way because Matt had tracked down the woman Ned might have gone off with.

She couldn't quite convince herself of that, not with the memory of last night's kiss so fresh in her mind that she could still feel his lips on hers.

He reached across to open the door as she approached, and she slid in, tossing the umbrella into the backseat.

"Good morning." His gaze lingered on her face for a moment, so warm that it brought a flush to her cheeks.

"Good morning to you, too." She smoothed back unruly curls, hoping he didn't see just how affected she was by his presence. "This is amazing news. I can't believe you found her so quickly."

"Once we had a name, it wasn't that hard." He pulled out onto the road. "There's an investigator the firm sometimes uses, so I put him onto it. Don't worry—he doesn't know why I was looking for her."

Worry was too constant a companion on this subject. She knew the truth was bound to come out, but she couldn't help wanting to delay that moment as long as possible.

"But if she ran away with Ned, he'd know—"

"She didn't," he said quickly.

She didn't know whether to be relieved or disappointed. "He's sure of that?"

He nodded, turning toward the drawbridge. "There's no mystery about it at all. Mr. and Mrs. Malloy went back to their home in Summerville after that summer on the island. They lived there until his death in the seventies. She moved to Charleston then, living first in a retirement community and now in a nursing home. They had one child, a daughter, who also lives in the city." He glanced at her. "If there had been any gap in the story, our investigator would have found it."

"So that was a dead end."

"Not necessarily." His eyes were focused on the traffic, giving her the freedom to study his strong, capable hands on the wheel, the firm line of his jaw, the tiny wrinkles at the corners of his eyes.

"What do you mean? If he didn't go away with her, we still don't know what happened to him."

"She might know. If Benny was right about the

relationship, she might be the one person who did know."

"Did?"

He shrugged. "Did. Does. As I told you, she's in a nursing home, apparently not expected to live long. Whether she's able to talk…"

"That's why you said we had to go right away." She'd wondered at the urgency in his voice when he'd called this morning. Now she knew.

He nodded, glancing at the screen of his GPS. "I just wish I knew how we were going to get in to see her."

"That part won't be too difficult. I've visited more nursing homes than I can count. It's part of growing up Southern, like visits to the cemetery. We'll need to make a stop to pick up some flowers, that's all." She smiled at his expression. "Trust me on this one."

The nursing home proved to be the one on the outskirts of Mount Pleasant, making things even easier than she'd predicted. Her mother had visited here regularly, bringing flowers and seasonal treats to elderly church members. A few minutes' chat with the nurse on duty at the desk, and they were soon pushing open the door to Mrs. Malloy's room.

The woman sleeping in the railed bed didn't bear much resemblance to the picture that had formed in Georgia's mind of the heroine of that wartime romance. But then, Ned, if he were still alive, would be eighty-four, and the woman he'd supposedly loved would be even older.

A faded wedding picture stood on the bedside table, and she moved closer to have a look. The woman had been a delicate beauty, with masses of fair hair and a fragile grace that had probably appealed to Ned's chivalrous instincts. The man had a square, red, bulldog face. He gripped his young bride with a possessive air.

She glanced from the photo to the woman in the bed. There were still traces of that fragile beauty in the worn face, like an echo of the vanished past.

Matt stood back from the bed, clearly uncomfortable. This was up to her, it seemed.

"Grace." She said the name softly, touching a thin, veined hand. "We've come to visit you. We brought you some flowers."

Eyelids flickered, then opened, and faded blue eyes attempted to focus. "Flowers," she murmured.

Georgia held the mixed bouquet closer, so that she could see and smell them. "Daisies and roses, with a little baby's breath. Shall I put them in a vase for you?"

A faint nod, which she took for yes. This part of the visit was familiar. She'd always found a vase and arranged the flowers while her mother made cheerful small talk, never acting bothered if there was no response.

Emulating her, Georgia chattered about the

flowers, about the weather, about the room while she fixed the flowers at the small sink and carried them to the bedside.

Grace smiled faintly, as if the aroma of the flowers touched some memory hidden deep in the recesses of her mind. "Who?" she whispered.

"I'm Georgia." She took the woman's hand again, her heart beating a little faster. "Georgia Bodine. I think you once knew my family, that summer you spent on Sullivan's Island, a long time ago."

She frowned, as if chasing an elusive memory.

"You'd better ask her directly," Matt said.

Georgia held the wasted hand in both of hers. "Ned Bodine," she said. "Do you remember him, Grace?"

For a moment there was nothing. Then the faintest trace of animation lit the woman's features. "Ned," she murmured. "Ned."

Georgia leaned closer. "Yes, Ned Bodine. Do you remember Ned? He loved you, I think."

For a moment a smile lingered on her lips. Then her brow furrowed, and she closed her eyes.

She was slipping off into whatever world she inhabited now. Georgia's heart wrenched.

Bless her, dear Lord. Ease her passage into Your presence.

"Grace?" She tried again. "Do you remember Ned?"

The only answer came from behind her as the door swung open.

"Who are you people? What are you doing in my mother's room?"

The woman who swept in moved protectively toward the bed, forcing Georgia to retreat. She didn't have her mother's beauty, but there was a faint resemblance between the faded creature on the bed and the erect, assertive sixty-something woman who stood next to her.

"I'm sorry to intrude, ma'am...." She hesitated, not sure of the daughter's name.

"Ms. Wilson," Matt said quietly. "I assume you're Beatrice Wilson. My name is Matthew Harper. I'm an attorney with Porter and Harper. This is Georgia Bodine."

"That doesn't explain what you're doing here," the woman said tartly.

Georgia exchanged glances with Matt. "I believe that your mother was acquainted with my great-uncle. We were hoping she might remember something about him. His name was Ned Bodine."

The woman knew his name. Georgia could see it in the sudden tensing of her body, in the quick, dismissing movement of one hand, as if she'd brush them away.

"My mother never knew anyone by the name. You'll have to leave. She's in no condition to have company."

"Please, Ms. Wilson." She held her hand out in appeal. "It's very important to my grandmother to find out what happened to Ned. If your mother remembers anything—"

"She doesn't." She clipped off the words, her gaze sliding away from Georgia's as she took her mother's hand in a protective grasp. "Please leave."

"But I just want—"

Matt touched her arm gently, and she could feel his sympathy through the light caress. He held out his card to Ms. Wilson. "Anything your mother knows or might have told you could be of great value. If you think of something, please believe we'd treat it with discretion."

She made no response, so he put the card down on the bedside table.

"If you're willing to talk to us later, I hope you'll call me."

She pressed her lips together for a moment, then shook her head.

"If only you'd let me—"

Matt grasped her elbow, piloting her out of the room before she could finish the sentence. The door swung shut behind them.

Georgia tried to shake him off, but he didn't loosen his grip. "I'm sure she knows something."

"And I'm just as sure that she's not going to tell you." He hustled her down the hallway. "You can't badger a dying woman, Georgia. Or her grieving daughter."

"But she knew…" She let that trail off. He was

right, of course. She couldn't let her need to help Miz Callie override common kindness. Miz Callie was the last person to want that.

She glanced at Matt. His face was set, and lines of tension radiated from his eyes. He moved so quickly that she could barely keep up with him.

"I don't think we need to run," she said mildly.

"I don't like nursing homes." He clipped off the words. "Let's get out of here."

His shuttered expression warned her. Her heart twisted. His wife—had she been in a nursing home, making this visit a painful reminder?

She didn't know, because Matt wouldn't, or couldn't talk about that. All she knew was what everyone knew—that his wife had died, and that it had nearly destroyed him.

He'd kissed her. He seemed to care about her. But he wouldn't let her into what was really important to him, and judging by the look on his face, she didn't think he ever would.

Chapter Fifteen

Georgia jogged slowly from the beach to the stairs that led up to Miz Callie's deck the next morning, stopping at the bottom to stretch. As the heat intensified, she'd had to get her run in earlier and earlier.

She'd had some vague hope that jogging along the beach in the morning light might clear her mind, but she was no nearer any decisions than she had been. Her own future was still a tangle that she couldn't seem to unravel. As for her grandmother's problem, the more they learned, the less they knew.

She'd looked up Ms. Wilson's phone number and address the night before, and a half-dozen times she'd reached for the phone. Each time, something held her back. She couldn't badger the woman when her mother was dying. But with the woman's death might go their last chance of learning the truth.

Matt clearly didn't want to pursue that angle any further. But was his opinion based on logic or emotion? She wasn't sure.

She glanced down the beach, shielding her eyes with her hand. There was Miz Callie, back from her turtle patrol, but where was Lindsay? The two of them had set off together when she'd left for her run.

Impelled by something that seemed amiss in the solitary figure, she trotted down to meet her grandmother.

"Hey, Miz Callie. What happened to Lindsay? I thought she was with you."

"She's down there at the turtle nest. She didn't want to come back yet." Her grandmother's eyes showed concern. "Somethin's ailing that child, but she wouldn't say what. You go, Georgia. Maybe she'll talk to you."

She put her arm around her grandmother's waist in a quick hug. "If she wouldn't tell you what's troubling her, she surely won't tell me."

Miz Callie patted her cheek, but her gaze was stern. "Don't you belittle yourself, Georgia Lee. Goodness, you're the one everyone wants to tell their troubles to. You go and try your luck with Lindsay. She needs you."

Still doubtful, she nodded. She certainly couldn't leave Lindsay there all alone. "I'll try."

She began to jog again, her legs protesting a little. Was her grandmother serious about people wanting to confide in her? She'd always considered that Miz Callie's role in the family, not hers.

Matt certainly didn't want to do any confiding in her.

The turtle nest came into view. Lindsay was a small, lonely figure, sitting with her arms wrapped around her knees next to the orange tape. She looked so desolate that for a moment Georgia's heart failed her.

Lord, that child is hurting so much. I don't feel qualified to help her, but there doesn't seem to be anyone else. Please, if this is Your will, guide my words. Let me bring her some comfort.

Lindsay didn't acknowledge her presence as Georgia jogged up and dropped to the sand next to her.

"Hey, Lindsay. Are you visiting with the baby turtles this mornin'?"

Lindsay turned her face away, as if looking at the nest, but not before Georgia had seen the traces of tears on her cheeks. Her heart clenched.

"It…it takes them a long time to hatch, doesn't it?"

"Quite a while." She searched her memory for the turtle lore her grandmother had planted there over the years. "I don't think they'll hatch out until later in the summer. Miz Callie will know. She'll watch for the signs."

Lindsay sat still, face averted. This was obviously not about turtles, but if she prodded, Lindsay would retreat further into her shell, protecting herself as one of the loggerheads would.

"That'll be their birthday," Lindsay said softly. "When they hatch."

"I guess so." She waited for more.

"Where will their mother be on their birthday?"

Georgia was ill-prepared to talk to the child about her mother. She'd done her best when it had come up the day of Lindsay's party, but obviously her best hadn't been good enough.

Please, Lord.

"She'll be out in the ocean. That's where her nature tells her to be, and that's where the baby turtles will go when they hatch. And then, when they're grown up and ready to lay their eggs, they'll come back to this same beach to make their nests, right back where they were born."

Those that survive, she added silently. Now was not the time for a lesson on how endangered the loggerhead turtles were.

"My mommy used to tell me the story about when I was born. How my daddy drove her to the hospital, and how they were so happy when they had a little girl." Lindsay rubbed her eyes with the heels of her hands. "When Mommy got sick, I prayed that Jesus would make her well. But He didn't."

It wasn't the time for a theology lesson, either;

she knew that instinctively. She had to say something that would comfort, but all she could feel was fear that she'd say the wrong thing.

Please, Father. Please give me the words.

"I know your mommy and daddy were the happiest people in the world when you were born." Now came the hard part, and she tested each word before she spoke. "I don't think anybody understands why sometimes people don't get well when we pray for them. But we know that Jesus loves us and will always be with us, no matter how sad or lonely we feel."

Lindsay swung to face her. "I miss her. Georgia, I miss Mommy so much."

Her heart seemed to crack as she put her arm around Lindsay's shoulders and drew her close. "Oh, honey, of course you miss her."

Lindsay burrowed her face into Georgia's chest. "I wanted to talk to Daddy about her, but I couldn't." Her voice was muffled.

Georgia held her tighter. "Why not, sugar?"

But she already knew. Matt held his grief so close that he couldn't let anyone in, not even his child.

"It might make him mad," she whispered.

"Not mad, Lindsay. Just sad, that's all. Sometimes it's hard to tell what someone else is feeling, but I know your daddy would never get mad at you for that."

Oh, Matt. Don't you see what you're doing? You're closing her out.

She smoothed her hand down the curve of Lindsay's back, feeling the fragility of tiny bones, the small shoulder blades like a bird's wings.

"How would it be if I went with you to tell your daddy that you want to talk about your mommy? Is he home this morning?"

Lindsay nodded. The movement seemed to bruise her heart. "I'm afraid," she whispered. "I don't want Daddy to be mad. Or sad. Maybe I shouldn't."

"I think you should." Conviction grew in her. Silence brought barriers between people. She knew. She and her mother were a great example of that.

Lindsay was motionless for a moment. Then she drew back. "Okay. If you promise you'll go with me."

Georgia stood, holding out her hand to Lindsay. "I promise."

Lindsay scrambled to her feet and took Georgia's hand. Together they started down the beach.

As they approached the house, Georgia's breath hitched. Was she doing the right thing?

She was doing the only thing. Someone had to help Matt see what his silence was doing to his daughter, and God had plopped the issue right in her lap.

Are You sure You've picked the right person for this job, Lord? You know how I am about confronting people. Hopeless, that's how. I quake inside. I run away.

If she'd longed for a sense that she could pass this off to someone else, she didn't get it. Come what may, she had to do this. And what was most likely to come was that Matt would be so furious that whatever existed between them would be extinguished in an instant.

She glanced at Lindsay as they started up the stairs together. One ponytail was slipping to the side, and the part in her hair was slightly crooked. The sight choked Georgia's throat with unshed tears. This vulnerable child deserved to have someone speak for her. This time there'd be no running away.

Lindsay tugged at the sliding glass door, and Georgia helped her push it back. Cool air floated out in greeting as they stepped inside.

Matt sat at the desk in the living room, a laptop open in front of him. At the sight of her, his eyebrows lifted in a question.

"Hi, Lindsay. I thought you were out checking turtle nests with Miz Callie."

Lindsay hesitated, and Georgia could feel the tension that gripped her. "I was. I...I..." She pressed her fingers against her shorts, seeming unable to go on.

Georgia placed a gentle hand on the child's shoulder. "Lindsay didn't want to leave the turtle nest, so my grandmother asked me to talk with her."

Concern darkened the steel blue of Matt's eyes.

He shoved his chair back and reached out a hand toward his daughter. "Lindsay? What's wrong?"

"I…" Lindsay tilted her face to Georgia, her gaze pleading. "I can't," she whispered.

"It's all right." She took a deep breath, hoping it would release the stranglehold around her throat, and uttered a wordless prayer. "Lindsay told me she wanted to talk to you about something, but she was afraid it might upset you."

"My daughter can talk to me about anything." But even as he said the words, he drew away from them, his body language saying exactly the opposite.

For Lindsay's sake, she had to go on. "She misses her mommy, and she needs to talk about her. To you."

Understand, Matt. Please understand.

Lindsay clung to her hand. Without it, she'd probably run from the room. That was exactly how Georgia felt, too.

As for Matt—she could sense the battle that raged within him, even if she didn't entirely understand it. Surely he could put his child's welfare ahead of his own feelings.

"Lindsay, honey." He reached for her then, took her hand, drew her close. "We can talk about Mommy if that's what you want." His voice was taut with strain, but it was gentle.

Cautiously, Lindsay reached up to pat his cheek. "Don't be sad, Daddy."

He managed a smile, dropped a kiss on her small palm. "I'll try not to be. Were you feeling sad about Mommy today?"

She nodded. "Sometimes I'm afraid I'm going to forget about her," she whispered. "I don't want to." She sounded panicked. "I don't want to forget."

"No, no, of course you don't." He put his arms around her, holding her close. "You won't forget. It's okay."

Georgia's throat closed with tears. This hurt him—she could feel it. But he was doing it. Maybe he needed this as much as Lindsay did.

"Remember how Mommy always told the story about how I was born? Every birthday she told me that story."

He smoothed his hand over her hair. "I remember," he said, his voice rough. "Do you want me to tell you?"

She nodded. "Can I get my baby book out to look at while you tell the story, just like me and Mommy did?"

"Sure you can." He released her, giving her a gentle push toward the stairs. "You run up and get it while I walk Georgia out."

"Okay." The smile that dawned on Lindsay's face was a delight to see. "Thank you, Georgia."

"You're welcome, sugar." She managed to hold her smile until the child turned away. Then all she wanted to do was run.

Matt was furious with her. Maybe he had a right to be. She turned and preceded him out to the deck and down the stairs.

But she'd done the right thing. No matter what it cost her, she'd done the right thing.

His tread was heavy on the steps. She could sense the weight of his emotion—the power of will that held it back until they were out of earshot of his daughter.

At the bottom of the steps, he stopped. "I suppose you think you had to do that."

It took all the courage she possessed to meet the grief and anger that clouded his eyes. "I'm sorry if that hurt you, but—"

"If?" The word exploded out of him.

Her cheeks burned. "All right. I knew it would be painful. But Lindsay was hurting, too. She confided in me." She shook her head, longing to reach him, not sure she knew how. "Don't you see, Matt? She is desperate to talk about her mother to someone, and there's no one here who knew her. No one but you."

His jaw clenched at the words, so tightly that it seemed it might break from the pressure. She quailed inside, waiting for an explosion.

It didn't come. Matt took one careful breath. Then another.

"I know you're trying to help. I appreciate that."

Encouraged, she longed to reach out and touch

him but didn't quite darc. "She needs you, Matt. She needs you to talk about her mother. If only you could share your grief—"

"No!" Matt grabbed the railing, the tendons of his forearms standing out. "That I can't do. Don't you understand?" He threw the words at her angrily.

Only her love for the little girl kept her from backing away. "No, I don't. Tell me. Or tell someone, if not me. You can't…"

The words trailed off. Who was she to give advice to someone about grieving? She couldn't even imagine the magnitude of his loss. But Lindsay—Lindsay she did understand. And Lindsay needed help.

"You know everything there is to know about my family, I think. And I don't even know how your wife died."

"Cancer." He spit the word out. "Jennifer died of cancer." He paused, but maybe having said that much made it easier for him to go on. "She was so strong, so brave. Her faith never wavered, right to the very end."

She didn't know what to say, and couldn't have said it if she had known.

He shrugged, his shoulders moving stiffly. "I thought my faith was strong, too, until I was finally alone after the funeral." He turned to her then. "You know what I did? I fell apart—acted like a total madman. Screamed, broke things, threw things, raged at God."

"Lindsay…" She whispered the name.

"Lindsay was with her grandparents."

Of course. Certainty built in her. "You wouldn't have done it if she had been there."

"You can't know that." Fury sparked from his eyes. "Don't you see? The only way I can be sure of keeping control is to shut it away." The anger faded, just a little, and he suddenly looked exhausted. "I'll do what I can to satisfy Lindsay, but I can't let go of my control."

"I'm sorry." She whispered the words, sorrow weighing heavily on her. "But I think you're wrong. I'd better go."

As she turned, he grabbed her hand, holding it tightly.

"Don't, Georgia." His voice was ragged. "I don't want to drive you away. I don't want to lose you. But just don't ask me to open my heart, because that's the one thing I can't do."

He was offering her something. It was there under the words. A relationship, but one that had strings attached.

Longing filled her heart. If only she could agree, keep silent, anything to preserve what they had.

But she couldn't. She wasn't the same person she'd been when she came back to the island. Somehow, through knowing him, through struggling to help Lindsay, through dealing with Miz Callie's problem, she'd become stronger.

Maybe God had led her through this for that purpose. She couldn't turn back now, no matter what it cost.

Love costs, Miz Callie had said. She was right.

"I'm sorry." She managed to keep her voice even, but it took an effort. "I can't settle for that. Not for myself, and not for you."

He didn't move. He let go of her hand, and his silence said more than words.

It was over. Feeling her heart splinter in her chest, she turned and walked away.

Chapter Sixteen

Georgia drew her car to a stop in front of Beatrice Wilson's house and hesitated, her hands trembling on the steering wheel. She hadn't called before coming, sure the woman would hang up at the sound of her voice.

Probably Ms. Wilson would slam the door instead, but she had to try. They were out of options. Beatrice Wilson's mother was the only person who might know what happened to Ned when he left Charleston all those years ago.

She'd failed with Matt, and she had a gaping hole in her heart as a souvenir of that encounter. Funny that it had taken this very real pain to show her that what she'd felt about the breakup with James had been nothing but damaged pride.

She took a breath, pressing her palms together to still their quivering. She couldn't do anything about

Matt, but maybe she could still salvage something from the wreckage for her grandmother. Georgia slid from the car and headed for the wrought-iron gate in the low brick wall that surrounded the house.

The gate pushed open at a touch, and she walked into a tiny courtyard. The two-story house, set endways to the street, its veranda facing the court-yard, was classic Charleston in style. A brick path led to the veranda, where the front door's frosted glass hid the interior. Breathing a silent prayer, Georgia reached for the shell-shaped knocker and let it fall.

A click of heels resounded faintly from inside, and then the door opened. Beatrice Wilson stared at her for a moment and then swung the door toward her.

Georgia caught it with her hand. She hadn't re-hearsed what she'd say, but the words seemed to spring to her lips.

"Please, Ms. Wilson. I know you're trying to protect your mother. I don't mean her any harm or embarrassment, I promise. Just give me five minutes. Then if you're not willing to talk to me, I'll never bother you or her again."

For a moment the woman stood frozen, her face strained, her eyelids red. Then she swung the door open. "You can come in, but it won't do you any good. My mother died early this morning."

A cold hand squeezed Georgia's heart as sorrow swept over her—for Ms. Wilson, for her mother and for Miz Callie, who would never know the truth.

"I'm sorry." She reached out impulsively to clasp the woman's hand as she stepped into the cool, tiled hallway. "I'm so sorry for your loss."

Ms. Wilson nodded, closing the door. The muscles in her neck worked. "It was expected, but it's still hard. Harder than I thought."

"I'm sorry," she said again. There didn't seem anything else to say. "I should go. I'm sure you have a great deal to do."

"Tell me first." Ms. Wilson's lips trembled, and she pressed them together. "What did you want from my mother?"

She knew something. Georgia was sure of it. She'd reacted to Ned's name before she threw them out of the room at the nursing home.

"Ned Bodine was my grandfather's older brother. He disappeared in 1942—left without telling anyone where he was going." She hesitated, but what point was there in evasion? "People believed he ran away rather than enlist. They called him a coward."

"Why are you interested in it now? What difference could it make to anyone?" The woman's gaze slid away from Georgia's and focused on an arrangement of pink roses on a marble-topped hall stand.

"My grandmother cares. She's starting to see her

friends pass away, and that's made her think of things she regrets—like never trying to prove that Ned wasn't the coward people thought him."

"Is she so sure of that?"

"Yes," she said instantly. "She is, and she's desperate to clear his name."

Still the woman didn't look at her. "What does that have to do with my mother?"

She hesitated, wondering whether she dared say what she knew, what she suspected, about Ned and Beatrice's mother. But again, what good would it do to hold it back?

"Your parents rented a house on Sullivan's Island that summer. People remember that Ned and your mother were…friends."

She flared up at that. "My mother was a kind person. People loved her."

"I'm sure they did," Georgia said gently. "My grandmother remembers a night when she found Ned standing in the dunes outside your parents' cottage. She remembers hearing your father shouting and the sound of a slap."

Beatrice Wilson stood perfectly still, but her hands twisted together as if they fought for control.

"We have no intention of making any of that public," Georgia said softly, pity filling her heart. "I just hoped that your mother might have remembered. Might have known why Ned went away the way he did. But I guess it's too late. Thank you for your time. And again, I'm sorry." She turned toward the door.

"Wait." For another instant the woman stood motionless, as if she'd surprised herself by the word. Then she spun and hurried through the archway into the parlor. In a moment she was back, holding something in her hand.

"When Mamma went into the nursing home, I sorted her things. I found these." She hesitated a moment. "I was going to burn them." She took a choking breath, and her eyes welled. "You were right about my father. Maybe this…" She thrust the papers toward Georgia. "Here. Take them."

They crackled in her fingers. Three envelopes: old, yellowed, the writing faded.

"Please go." The woman looked at the end of her rope. "I hope—I hope they have the answers you're looking for."

Georgia stepped outside and hurried to the car, forcing herself to wait until she was safely inside. She opened the first envelope, her fingers fumbling, breath hitching.

A few minutes later she sat back in her seat, wiping tears from her eyes. She understood now why Ned had left, but whether that would be enough to clear his name, she couldn't guess.

Matt resisted the temptation to put his hands over his ears. It wouldn't help. Nothing would block out the sound of the Bodine clan in full crisis mode.

Georgia had said something once about her family's penchant for noisy interference in each other's business. He saw what she meant. No wonder she was so reluctant to confront them.

Miz Callie sat in her rocking chair while agitated voices swirled, her face set. She wasn't even attempting to explain.

Maybe she had it right. Maybe it was necessary to let them run out of steam, and then they'd be ready to listen.

But he doubted it.

All three of Miz Callie's sons and their wives were here, along with Georgia's brother Adam and her cousin Amanda. He wasn't quite sure why they'd been dragged along—maybe because the older generation blamed them for helping.

Amanda, sitting between her father and Georgia's father, was trying to play peacemaker, but judging by the spark in her eyes, she'd rather just yell at them. Adam stood behind his grandmother, immovable as a boulder, letting the torrent of voices roll around him.

"Don't you have anything to say for yourself?" Ashton Bodine demanded.

Matt realized that was directed at him. Somewhat to his surprise, the talk died down for his answer.

Not that they'd like it.

"Miz Callie is my client," he said. "I'm carrying out her wishes, and I'll continue to do that."

The clamor fell on his ears again. He'd warned Georgia that the further the paperwork went, the more likely someone would leak the plan. That was exactly what had happened.

Georgia should be here, but he was just as glad she wasn't. She would hate this.

Pain wrapped around his heart at the thought of her. He'd hurt her. He hadn't intended to, but he had.

He longed to see her again, to try and make amends, but how could he? She asked the impossible of him.

The front door opened. Georgia stood there, staring at the scene in front of her. For an instant he saw panic in her eyes, and then her fight to control it.

"Georgia!"

Ignoring her mother's exclamation, Georgia crossed the room to her grandmother and bent to kiss her cheek. "Are you all right?" she asked, as if there were no one else in the room.

"I am." Miz Callie patted her cheek. "But better for having you here, sugar."

"Georgia Lee, I think you'd better explain your part in this." Her father's voice held a note of command.

Other voices lifted as her aunts and uncles chimed in, demanding answers.

Matt saw Georgia exchange glances with her brother and her cousin. But not with him, and the omission nicked his heart. She straightened, holding her grandmother's hand.

"As soon as y'all can get quiet, I do have something to say."

The sudden silence was as weighty as a breaker crashing. Her father blinked. "All right, Georgia Lee. We're listening."

"First of all, Miz Callie asked me to do something for her. She asked me to find out what really happened to Ned Bodine."

There was a strangled noise from one of the uncles, and she shot him a look so stern that he shut up probably from sheer amazement.

"The truth, not just what everyone says. The truth that Miz Callie believes—that Ned Bodine wasn't a coward."

Her father cleared his throat. "Mamma..." His voice gentled, "I'm touched you believe that, but after all this time, no one can possibly find out—"

"But they can," Georgia said, her voice firmer than he'd ever heard it. "I did."

Now he was gaping like the rest of them.

Georgia looked down at her grandmother, patting her hand. "It was just as you thought. Ned was in love with the woman who rented the next cottage that summer. He wanted desperately to protect her from her abusive husband."

"If they ran away," Miz Callie began, voice trembling.

Georgia stroked her hand. "It wasn't that. When Ned realized that she wouldn't let him help her, he decided he had to go away. To join up, as his friends did."

"We didn't find any records," Matt reminded her.

"No." Her gaze finally met his, cautious, guarded, as if just looking at him might hurt her. "Because he didn't enlist under his own name."

Her father was shaking his head. "Georgia, I appreciate your trying to help your grandmother, but you can't know this."

She held up several yellowed sheets of paper. "I have proof—the letters Ned wrote to her that summer. The last one says it all." Carefully, she unfolded the brittle paper. "He tells her that he's leaving, and why. And he says that since his father has spent so much time telling him that he's a disgrace to the Bodine name, he won't be using it." A single tear dropped on the paper, and she carefully blotted it away. "As far as we know, no one ever heard of Ned Bodine again."

"Georgia…" Miz Callie breathed her name, eyes sparkling with tears.

Georgia pressed the letters into her hand. "For you."

She'd done it. She'd obviously gone to the Wilson woman again, and she'd pulled off something he'd thought impossible. Not only that, but she'd stood up to her entire family. His heart swelled with pride. Pride, and regret that in the end, he hadn't helped her.

Her parents and aunts and uncles stared at her in amazement. Her brother reached over to envelop her in a huge congratulatory hug, and she turned her face into his shirt.

A pang shot through Matt, headed straight for his heart. He wanted it to be him comforting her, celebrating with her. But he'd forfeited any possibility of that.

"Astonishing," murmured Brett, Amanda's father. "But y'all know people are still going to talk. We can't very well put his letter in the newspaper as proof."

There was a murmur, maybe of agreement. Georgia turned toward them again. "There's nothing to be ashamed of."

Silence for a moment, and then Georgia's mother rose.

"Let them talk." She held out her hand to her daughter. "We're Bodines. If people talk, we'll hold our heads a little higher, won't we, honey?" The smile she gave Georgia held love and pride.

Georgia took her hand, stepped into her embrace. The others, following Delia's lead, clustered around. The Bodines were a single unit again, surrounding Georgia.

Excluding him. That was the way it should be. Georgia deserved the best. She deserved a man who could offer her a whole heart. He couldn't.

He turned and slipped quietly out.

Chapter Seventeen

Finally the family had gone. Georgia was alone on the beach. The sun slipped toward the horizon, and the last of the day's beachgoers had left. She really was alone.

She should feel lost. Whatever might have been with Matt was gone. She'd finished the job Miz Callie had set for her. But instead of feeling lost, she felt a sense of release. Of freedom. She no longer had to make decisions based on her sense of failure.

She could stay here. The idea took hold, strong as the incoming tide. She didn't have to worry about putting space between herself and her family's expectations. She could stay where her roots ran deep. Even though the love she'd hoped for with Matt could never be, she could build a satisfying life. Surely someone in Charleston needed an employee with her experience.

Her steps grew lighter, quicker, and her mind raced with the decision made. She'd go back to Atlanta and give up the apartment—that was the first thing. She'd spend a couple of days winding up things there, then come back and launch into a serious job hunt. Maybe Amanda would know of something.

She should tell Miz Callie. But first—her steps had taken her as far as Matt's house. Standing on the beach, the incoming tide sending ripples chasing her feet, she looked at the house.

Lights were on, glowing behind the drapes. He was there. Maybe, before she moved on, there was something still to be said between them, no matter how much it might hurt to be with him again.

By the time she'd disentangled herself from her family earlier, he'd gone. She hadn't thanked him yet. If he hadn't tracked down Grace Malloy, she'd never have gotten her hands on the letters, and Miz Callie would still be wondering. She owed him for that, at least.

Her feet felt rooted in the sand. Giving herself a shake, she started walking toward the house. *No more hiding, Georgia Lee. You're finished with that. God has set you free.*

She reached the steps and went steadily up them, then knocked on the glass door. In a moment Matt pushed it back, looking surprised to see her and a bit guarded as well.

"Georgia. I wasn't expecting you." He stepped back, gesturing her inside.

She nodded. A quick glance showed her Lindsay was nowhere in sight. They were alone.

She sucked in a breath. Her heart was beating faster than a hummingbird's wings, and something seemed to grip her throat.

Matt stood waiting, the newspaper he'd apparently been reading dangling from his hand. When he realized he still held it, he tossed it onto the coffee table.

Another breath might help. Breathing was always a good idea.

"I came over to thank you." She stumbled a little on the words, but she got them out. "If it weren't for you, I'd never have found the truth about Ned."

He nodded. "You're welcome, but you're the one who did it. And your uncle was right. It's not the sort of thing you'll be able to tell the public."

"My grandmother's happy. That's the only thing that really matters. And Amanda and Adam are bubbling with ideas for figuring out where he enlisted and what name he used."

His eyes grew remote. "It'll be easier on you now that the family is on board with this. You'll be heading back to Atlanta any day now, I suppose."

"I'm driving up tomorrow, but—"

"No!" A wail was followed by the thud of bare feet on the stairs. Lindsay, pajama-clad, rushed down the steps, across the room and threw herself at Georgia.

Georgia knelt to catch the child in her arms. "Hey, what's this? It's all right. I—"

"You can't go! You can't." Lindsay got the words out between sobs that were nearly hysterical. "I love you, Georgia. If you go, I won't have anybody to talk to."

Georgia cradled her in her arms, afraid to look at Matt for fear of the condemnation she'd see there. She petted the child, murmuring softly. "You have Miz Callie, and you have Daddy. Besides—"

"Daddy doesn't want to talk about Mommy." She shook her head so wildly that her braids snapped to and fro. "He doesn't. He doesn't love her any more!"

"Lindsay—"

Before she could say more, Matt dropped to his knees next to her. Instead of the anger she expected, his eyes were filled with tears.

"Lindsay, no. That's not true." He tried to take her from Georgia, but she clung like a barnacle. "Honey, listen to me. I love you. And I love Mommy. Didn't we talk about her when we looked at your baby book?"

"You didn't want to." She threw the words at him. "I know you didn't want to. You just did it cause Georgia told you to."

Georgia winced. What could she do or say that would mend this? *Please, Lord.*

But it wasn't her Lindsay needed to hear from now. It was Matt.

"Lindsay, listen." He took her face between his hands, turning it so that she had to look at him, had to see the tears that were running down his face. "When your mommy died, that was the worst thing that ever happened to me. I've been afraid to let you see how much it hurts me. I was afraid it would scare you."

That caught Lindsay's attention. She looked at him closely. Then she reached out one small hand and wiped at his tears.

"It's all right, Daddy. I'm not scared. You can cry if you want to."

For an instant Georgia thought Matt would shatter into a million pieces. Then he pulled his daughter into his arms. He held her close, his shoulders shaking, and their tears mingled.

Georgia struggled to her feet, trying to control her emotions. They were going to be all right. This time, Matt wasn't holding anything back.

Thank You, Father. Thank You for this.

Struggling to see the way through her own tears, she left them alone.

Georgia kissed her grandmother's cheek the next morning. Juggling a suitcase and the lunch Miz Callie had insisted on packing her, she started down the front steps to her car.

And stopped. Matt stood next to the car, obviously waiting for her.

"Hi." She went the rest of the way, busying herself with putting the bag and lunch in the back so she didn't have to look at him. "Is everything okay?"

"Fine." His smile broke through, erasing the lines of tension in his face. "Lindsay and I are both much better. I think I have you to thank for that."

She shook her head, looking anywhere but at him, because if she did, she might start to cry. "It wasn't my doing. Lindsay's the one who broke through."

"That's exactly what it was. Breaking through." He stood very close, so that she was caught between the car and his body. "I thought if I opened my heart, the grief would shatter me. Instead..." He stopped, and she heard the hitch in his breath. "Instead I found that opening it was the only thing that could heal me."

"I'm glad," she murmured. Inadequate. Words were inadequate.

"Georgia, don't go." He spoke in a sudden rush of feeling, grabbing her hand and gripping it tight. "Please, don't go away."

"I—"

"Wait, let me explain." He touched her lips gently with his finger, and she felt his touch run straight to her heart. "I'm sorry. So sorry for the way I acted.

You were right all along, and I kept trying to shut you out." His fingers fanned against her cheek. "I think God sent you here for that reason—because I wouldn't listen to anyone or anything else, including Him."

Thank You, Lord, she said silently. *Thank You.*

"I want to give life another chance," he said, his voice soft and low. "If you'll help me, I think I can make it."

She dared to look at him then. Love filled his eyes—love and hope that seemed to grow as he read what was in her face.

"You'll stay?" he breathed.

"I'll come back," she said. "I wasn't going to Atlanta to stay, just to close things up. My life is here."

With you. She wouldn't say the words, not yet. But when his lips claimed hers in a kiss, they both knew the truth.

It would take time—time to finish grieving, time for Lindsay to think of her as a parent. She slid her arms around Matt, feeling the strong, solid worth of him as he held her close.

She'd wait as long as she had to. But it would be worth it, because she knew they'd be a family in the end.

Epilogue

Georgia leaned against Matt's shoulder as they sat in the dunes. The sun had slid below the horizon, and the reds and oranges that had painted the sky faded slowly to deep purple. The waves murmured gently as night drew in.

"Hey, wake up, you two." Miz Callie stood a few feet away, next to an excited Lindsay. "This is the real thing. The babies are hatching."

Georgia scrambled to her feet and knelt by the nest. "You're sure?"

Matt squatted next to her, grasping her hand. "I think she knows."

The shallow, concave depression in the sand seemed to deepen as they watched.

"They're coming, they're coming!" Lindsay danced up and down with excitement. "They're really hatching after we waited forever!"

"Only a couple of months," Matt reminded her.

So much had changed in that time that Georgia could hardly get her mind around it. She glanced down at the diamond winking on her finger.

"This one's for real," Matt had whispered when he put it there. "I'm not James. You won't find it easy to get rid of me."

"I won't ever want to," she'd replied, heart so full of love that it seemed to expand in her chest.

Now she looked across the moving sand at the child who would be her daughter. The love she had for Lindsay was so strong that it continually astonished her.

"Georgia, look, look! The sand is bubbling!"

Lindsay leaned so far over the nest that she nearly fell in. Miz Callie grabbed her.

"That's what we call a boil, remember? They'll all pop out in a big bunch."

"Will they know which way to go?" Lindsay held on to Miz Callie, looking at her with worried eyes.

"'Course they will. All the house lights are off along the beach, and look at the way the moon is shining on the water. They'll head straight for the ocean, mark my words. And if any of them get lost, we'll be right here to help them."

Georgia glanced up, finding Matt's face very close. "You know, I think she might be more excited about getting Miz Callie as a grandmother than getting me as a mother."

He dropped a kiss on the tip of her nose. "We're both very lucky to get you, and we know it," he murmured. "God has been very good to us."

"Yes. He has." She glanced out at the water moving darkly under the shimmering path of the moon. Sea oats rustled in the breeze. A few faint stars had begun to shine.

Miz Callie's favorite verse drifted through her mind.

When I think of the heavens that Thou hast established, the moon and the stars, which Thou hast ordained...

"His love is overwhelming." Matt's hand tightened on hers. "Look. Here comes one."

A tiny snout broke through the sand. Then, like a pot boiling over, the hatchlings burst out into the cool night air, scrambling over one another in their hurry. They began their rush to the sea, following the instinct God had given them.

"Quick, quick!" Lindsay shrieked. "We have to keep them safe while Miz Callie counts them coming out of the nest."

They fanned out on either side of the moving wave of tiny turtles that scrambled over every obstacle in their fierce need to reach the sea. The moon made a silvery path for them, and Lindsay dashed alongside, face intent as she guarded them.

My place, Georgia thought as she shepherded a tiny turtle toward the waves. My place, my people, my destiny. She looked at Matt, helping his daughter chase off a ghost crab with designs on a hatchling. My love.

Thank You, Father. Thank You.

The first of the babies reached the waves, others following, their swimming reflexes kicking in. They would soon be safe in the ocean, where they belonged.

In thirty years or so, God willing, the females would return to lay their eggs on this beach again. She glanced at her grandmother. Miz Callie would be gone by then, but she had already passed the torch. A new generation of turtle ladies would take her place, safeguarding God's creation as she had taught them.

* * * * *

Dear Reader,

Thank you for choosing to read the first book in my new Love Inspired miniseries about the Bodine family of South Carolina. I hope you'll enjoy getting acquainted with the big, loving brood as they find love and begin new families.

It was a pleasure to set these stories in and around Charleston, one of my very favorite places. Readers familiar with the area will recognize some sites, although others have been created particularly for the story. Sullivan's Island Elementary School, which Lindsay will attend in the book, actually exists. My granddaughter goes there, and it's every bit as excellent as my characters say!

I hope you'll let me know how you felt about this story, and I'd love to send you a signed bookmark or my brochure of Pennsylvania Dutch recipes. You can write to me at Steeple Hill Books, 233 Broadway, Suite 1001, New York, NY 10279; e-mail me at www.martaperry.com.

Blessings,

Marta Perry

QUESTIONS FOR DISCUSSION

1. Can you understand the difficulty Georgia experienced in coming home, feeling as if she'd failed? Have you ever struggled to deal with a major life change like this? If so, how did God and other people help you with it?

2. Georgia's natural reaction is always to avoid confrontation at any cost. Did you empathize with her?

3. Georgia finds that everyone in her family has an opinion as to what she should do. Has this ever happened to you? How do you sort out God's calling from the demands of others?

4. Matthew struggles with his need to be both father and mother to his daughter. Have you ever experienced doubt about your ability as a parent? Has God helped you to gain insight?

5. The depth of his grief over his wife's death caused Matthew to doubt God. Has anything ever caused you to doubt God? What do you do during those times when you can't seem to feel His guidance?

6. The Scripture verse for this story has been a favorite of mine since childhood, and it never fails to comfort me to think that the God who created the universe cares for me. Do you have a verse that comforts you in this way? What is it, and why does it have this effect on you?

7. Georgia finds that she has to confront Matthew, initially over her grandmother, and later over Lindsay, even though she secretly feels she's a coward about confronting people. What gives her the courage to do so?

8. How does Lindsay express her grief over her mother's death in the story? How do you think Matthew should have handled it?

9. Georgia's grandmother longs to find out the truth about the past. Do you think it's always a good idea to do that?

10. Did you sympathize with Miz Callie about the changes she wanted to make in her life? Did you understand her children's apprehension about them?

11. How do you think grown children can balance their need to help elderly relatives with the older generation's need to remain independent?

12. Do you understand the difficulty Georgia faces in trying to help Lindsay communicate with her father? Have you ever been put in a buffer situation between two people you love? If so, how did you deal with it?

13. Which character in the story did you feel was living the most Christlike life? Why?

14. What did it take to bring Matthew to the point that he could open his heart again?

15. Some people, like Miz Callie, seem to have a special bond with nature. How does that fit into God's plans for the world He created?

Private investigator Wade Sutton plans to hightail it out of Dry Creek long before December 25. The town holds too many *unmerry* memories. Until he's asked to watch over a woman in danger, a woman whose faith changes him forever.

Turn the page for a sneak preview of
SILENT NIGHT IN DRY CREEK
by Janet Tronstad.
Available in October 2009
from Love Inspired®

Wade wished he had never come back to Dry Creek. Or, since he had come back, he wished people hadn't been so kind to him. Barbara making that cake for him was putting him off his game. And then Jasmine—usually he didn't have any trouble taking a tough line with a suspect. But then, he'd never been tempted to kiss a suspect before.

He watched Jasmine's back as she walked to the table. She was ramrod straight and angry with him. He knew he'd come on too strong, but it was either that or forgetting everything he knew about law enforcement and refusing to believe she could be responsible for anything.

As a lawman he had to consider all the possibilities, and it was hard to forget that Lonnie had been her partner. She could have sent him a coded message that in some way had helped him escape from prison, or at least given him an incentive to risk everything to get outside.

He wished he knew how to look into the heart of a person so he would know what Jasmine was thinking. Was she as innocent as she looked, or as guilty as she had been the first time she was convicted of a crime? He knew better than most how many ex-cons fell back into theft. He was often the one who took them in the second time around and listened to their sorry excuses.

"I gave you the biggest piece of cake," Barbara said as he sat down at his place at the table.

"Thank you." Wade smiled. It was the cake of his childhood fantasies, and he was going to have to force himself to eat it. All he wanted to do was take Jasmine home and then park his car at the end of the lane to her father's place. Why did she have to be tied up with Lonnie? Why couldn't she be a nice, ordinary woman like Barbara here? Carl never had to worry about arresting *her*.

Wade felt the smoothness of the cake on his tongue and the sweet tang of the raspberry filling. He smiled up at Barbara and thanked her again for the cake. The two kids at the table were smacking their lips and demanding more, just as Wade would be doing if he wasn't so troubled.

Then he looked down the table and saw his dear friend Edith. She wouldn't be happy about him keeping an eye on anyone. It was clear the older woman was very fond of Jasmine. That, of course, was the problem with being a lawman and trying to have friends. He liked things black and white with no shades of gray. He didn't want to have feelings for the suspect.

By doing his job, he was going to upset Jasmine and everyone else in Dry Creek. For the first time since he'd driven into town, he missed the barren feel of his apartment in Idaho Falls. He knew who he was there.

It didn't take long for Wade to leave the Walls' house, with Jasmine walking in front of him. The night was cold. Jasmine wrapped her arms around her body to keep warm and hurried to his car. He was still nursing that leg of his, so he went more slowly than she did. He made it in good time, though, and as he opened the car door for her, she nodded her thanks and slid into the passenger seat.

The first thing Wade did after he got into the car was to move the dial up on the heater. Snowflakes were just starting to fall, but they were scattered enough that he could clear them away with his windshield wipers.

He silently turned his car around and started down the sheriff's lane. The car lights shone on the falling snow, making the flakes look like pinpricks in the darkness.

"You don't think Lonnie would do something to my father, do you?" Jasmine asked. She looked up at him with eyes full of worry. "Lonnie's not very stable. I wouldn't want anyone around here to be hurt by him."

Wade shrugged. "With all you'd inherit if Elmer were out of the picture—"

Jasmine gasped. "I don't care about the money."

"Lonnie might."

That turned her quiet. He didn't want her to worry, though.

"He won't even have the chance to get close to anyone," Wade assured her. "We'll have the feds all over the place by tomorrow. Lonnie has a better chance of breaking in to Fort Knox than he has of sneaking into Dry Creek."

Wade hoped he wasn't lying. He had no idea what the feds would do. And they might have some completely different theories as to why Lonnie had broken out of prison. It might have nothing at all to do with Jasmine or anyone in Dry Creek.

"You'll be safe," Wade said as he opened his door.

He walked around to the passenger door and opened it. Wade stood by the open car door and watched as Jasmine pulled her coat closer to her body. She wasn't making any move to walk toward the house and he wasn't making any move to let her. Finally Wade reached out and touched her cheek. It was soft and a little damp. She must have been crying when she'd been huddled against the door on the drive out here.

"It'll be okay," he whispered to her as he brought his hand down.

"I'm fine," she said.

He nodded with a slight smile. "I know."

Wade had never kissed a suspect, but he would have done it now if he hadn't thought it would make Jasmine cry even more. She was barely hanging on, and he needed to leave her with her dignity.

"I'll be parked at the end of Elmer's lane if you need me," Wade said as he stepped back from the door. Snow was falling in earnest now, but in his trunk he had a heavy sleeping bag that he used on stakeouts like this. "I'll come to the door in the morning, before I go over to my grandfather's."

"You can't sleep outside all night. It's freezing out here. I'll leave the kitchen door unlocked in case you need to come inside."

"Don't leave anything unlocked. I'll duck into the barn if I need to."

Jasmine nodded.

Wade watched her walk to the kitchen door and go inside the house. Only then did he head back to the driver's door. He wondered if he'd get any sleep tonight. He was losing his edge. The next thing he knew, he was going to be offering pillows to everyone he arrested and wishing them sweet dreams. When had he turned into a soft touch?

He waited for the light to go out in the kitchen before he started his drive down the lane. He already felt lonely.

* * * * *

*Will Jasmine give Wade reason to call
Dry Creek home again?
Find out in
SILENT NIGHT IN DRY CREEK
by Janet Tronstad.
Available in October 2009
from Love Inspired®*

Love Inspired ®
SUSPENSE
RIVETING INSPIRATIONAL ROMANCE

These contemporary tales
of intrigue and romance
feature Christian characters
facing challenges to their faith...
and their lives!

**Four new Love Inspired Suspense titles are
available every month wherever books are
sold, including most bookstores, supermarkets,
drug stores and discount stores.**

Steeple
Hill ® ·

Visit:
www.steeplehillbooks.com

LISUSDIR08